The Feud at Broken Man

Lord Harry Lacey, the youngest son of an English aristocrat, has run away from debts at home to start a new life in America, using his skills with horses and guns to make a living as he journeys west to Colorado. Then he decides to give up his guns and start a new life as a public speaker in the new settlements where he believes people will be keen to experience culture.

However, arriving in Broken Man en route for Denver, Lord Harry witnesses a young girl being wounded in crossfire, and quickly learns that the town is being torn apart by a feud. Seeing an opportunity to do something useful, he tries to influence local leaders to resolve the situation – only to find that some disputes can only be settled with a gun.

The Feud at Broken Man

Frank Callan

A Black Horse Western

ROBERT HALE

© Frank Callan 2018
First published in Great Britain 2018

ISBN 978-0-7198-2604-7

The Crowood Press
The Stable Block
Crowood Lane
Ramsbury
Marlborough
Wiltshire SN8 2HR

www.bhwesterns.com

Robert Hale is an imprint
of The Crowood Press

Typeset by
Derek Doyle & Associates, Shaw Heath
Printed and bound in Great Britain by
CPI Group (UK) Ltd, Croydon, CR0 4YY

1

The stage was now finally well into Colorado and the occupants inside were exhausted, thirsty and ratty. Altercations could easily have been ignited by a jibe, a criticism or any passing remark which could have been taken the wrong way. A fat middle-aged man in a dark jacket and striped trousers had complained for the first forty miles of the present leg of their long journey; he had moaned about the small noisy child who squealed and cried at every jolt of the vehicle; her mother soothed, comforted, offered food and then finally she and her child had slept, huddled up to each other. There was a tall man who was clearly a country man, a man used to handling steers and leather: young, raw-faced and weather-beaten, with a sour expression. Then there was an old couple, heading west to visit their daughter who worked in Broken Man.

Finally, filling a corner, with his long legs struggling to find a resting place where they would not irritate any of the fellow passengers, there was Lord Harry Lacey. He was wearing a white shirt, dark trousers and some ex-army issue boots; his fair hair was long and stringy, and his face, hairy and weather-beaten, skulked beneath a battered hat. He had piercing blue eyes and was well over six feet tall, and so the young mother couldn't avoid looking at him when they all boarded the stage, and he smiled when he saw her glances, tipping his hat and giving his name: 'Lord Harry Lacey, Ma'am, a pleasure to make your acquaintance.'

She had blushed slightly and looked away. But the other passengers had noted the name. The old man had asked, 'Excuse me, mister, but you have an English voice under the Yankee one, to match that lordship you mention. You a new arrival from the old country, and are you actually a lord?'

'Oh, it's my professional name, see. Every legal contractor seems to have one. I have friends called Handy, Navaho and Captain, and no, I've been this side of the great ocean for three years, sir.'

'Legal contractor?' the old man's wife had asked.

'Oh, I'm a bookish sort of man, sir. I earn my corn by lecturing. I like to think that I bring a little East Coast conversation out here where folk are making a new land, a good, pure land.'

The other passengers wanted to have this clarified, but the old man knew what the words meant and he whispered in his wife's ear: 'He's lying . . .

6

he's a bounty hunter . . . man's a hired killer . . . see, he has that look. I seen it a thousand times. Under the smooth talking he's a ruthless killer.'

Harry knew that the whole company had heard this whisper, but he pretended not to notice. Anyway, he decided that some conversation would help remove the boredom.

'Look folks, we been together a long time, and only spoken a word or two. You all heading for Broken Man?'

The fat man said, 'Certainly. On business. There's a whole bunch of possibilities out in Colorado.'

The countryman smiled, 'Mister . . . I'm going to meet my woman!'

The others gave little words of happiness and congratulation, and the little girl asked if he was getting married. 'Well, that's what I'm pinning my hopes on, sweety . . . wish me luck!' Now they all clapped hands and the old lady tapped his arm.

'What about you, mister . . . you going to do some chin-wagging, I reckon?' the fat man asked.

'Oh yes. Most certainly. Broken Man has a fine literary society . . . word about it has spread far and wide.'

There were more whispers, and this time, Harry couldn't make out what was being said. So he tilted his hat and pretended to sleep, all the while listening to the tittle-tattle. In his head, the man's remarks about bounty-hunting rolled around in his brain. The word was a torment to him because yes,

7

he had done some man-hunting, among a dozen other jobs, since he arrived in New York three years back. He had soon learned that in this new world a man had to swallow pride and self-respect at first, just to put a claw in the hard land that promised so much but tended to wrench the guts out of any weak man.

'Only one little problem in Broken Man. . . .' This was the fat man again, 'There's a sheriff who seems to make enemies real easy, and the richest man around hates his guts. I heard that the lawman killed the rancher's brother. Surprised it's not led to a showdown yet.'

'Soon will,' the young man said, 'I can feel it in my bones. It's gonna come to a head.'

Harry Lacey listened closely but said nothing. He knew all about life with a gun, and he knew how places tended to get split apart. This trip out west was his testing of new ground. He had heard the stories of how life was lived out there, but now he wanted to see for himself, and maybe help to steady the ship in what were, according to reports and the newspapers, stormy times now, as the war was left behind and the race for land went on apace.

He had tried and tested any number of ways of life, but finally he had seen that violence gets more violence, and what the new country needed more than bullets was some refined behaviour, much as had been around him back home in Norfolk, where his father, Lord Kelvie, had made sure that the tough lives of his workers had enjoyed regular doses of singing, dancing and musical recitals. His father had believed in cultivating something he called sensibility, and Lord Harry believed in it. The problem was, he had never spoken the word since leaving the East for the less polite societies in the mid-West. Now here he was, venturing out further, expecting any minute to hear the sound of robbers or savages.

But he was brought back into the present world and the stage when a voice said, 'Mister, need a drink?'

It was the young man who had a marriage proposal running through his head. Now he whispered as he offered the bottle to Harry. 'Joe Dane, sir, at your service. Sir, I have to tell you . . . as you clearly don't know this . . . Broken Man means trouble.'

Harry was fully awake now. 'Trouble? How?'

'Well, the thing is you see, the sheriff and a character called Carney don't see eye to eye, and what's worse, they've been at each other's throats for a good year or so now, and there's men taking sides. I just thought you ought to know, sir. Matters will shortly come to a head.'

'How do you know that?'

'Well, sir, because I'm Joe Dane and I know these things.' He tapped his nose and gave a dark, menacing smile.

The old man sat up and called out, 'Ah, nearly there . . . I see the main street yonder, folks!'

The travellers began packing bags and checking

pockets. The mother and child sang a little song. Up above, the driver's voice cried out, 'Broken Man, Colorado, good people. Prepare to put on armour!'

Everyone laughed, but it was forced. Harry could sense the anxiety behind the smiles. He thought to himself, as the stage pulled up and the brakes squealed, *I'm a man without a weapon and I'm a few hundred miles west of reliable law.*

His information from the optimistic bachelor was not wrong. After Harry gathered his bags and let some time pass as the other travellers dispersed, he was aware of some kind of disturbance up the street.

'It's Jemmy's dog and it's gotten the mad head ... come quick!' That's what Harry heard, and then he saw the panic running through all four streets of Broken Man. The voice that announced this was not located – it just came from some corner somewhere, and then other voices took up the cry. Soon every drunkard, cow hand, loafer, merchant and bar tender was out in the streets looking for the dog. They didn't have to wait long. A great solid mastiff came scooting across by the sheriff's office and started howling.

'It's black as hell and carries death!' someone yelled. 'Git inside you folk, less you wanna die!' From all directions came cries of 'Mad as hell dog!' and 'hyderphobee!'

Sheriff Squint McCoy scrambled out, putting on his holster and in danger of shooting a hole in his foot as he had half a hand on his Colt. As he did this, the hound ran into The False Start saloon and there were screams of panic.

'Don't shoot, you'll put some hot lead into a human body!' said Happen Boodle, the owner, the foremost businessman of the town. He had run out to see what was happening, and then had gone to a drawer and brought out his mad-stone, a weapon reserved for emergencies; he grasped it firmly in his hand, so its powers could be working in case the teeth of the cur got sunk into him. His customers went under tables or ran into other rooms and slammed doors. The poor creature galloped outside again and Sheriff McCoy pulled out his gun, and pointed it at the beast – but at the instant he pulled the trigger, it ran towards two ladies who were just coming out of the general store, and the bullet splintered a square of the door frame. The ladies shrieked and fell flat on the ground, yelping like stuck pigs.

Harry was watching all this from behind a huge water-barrel, and since he had abandoned his guns, he had never felt more helpless. Kids now flooded out into the high sun of the summer day. They were mostly the rabble, the horde of offspring from Elias Hole's benighted family in their wreck of a home. In seconds, the rabble had cornered the dog, and its vicious teeth were out, ready for some gut-chewing work as the brood threw sticks at it and swore to high heaven.

Elias Hole then appeared, a thick-set man as tall as a lynching tree with his hair down to his waist and his beard tucked into his belt. He had a spade, and he advanced on the hound with the alacrity of a scared rabbit. Ploughing through his rabble, he slammed the spade down on the cornered cur and there was one pitiful moan just before the creature went down and stirred no more.

But Sheriff McCoy missed this and had only one thing on his mind: to shoot the dog. He walked briskly to the rabble, going by the heart-stopping howlings of the animal, and directed his gun at the source of the howl, just at the instant that Elias Hole entered the fray. Fortunately, the sheriff was no expert with a revolver and he hit a water trough. But Elias Hole was not skilled in constructive thinking, and he strode towards McCoy, spade in hand and murder in his heart.

'Stop him! Stop that Hole!' screamed Happen Boodle, and a crowd of assorted citizens ran out to pile on top of Hole before he could swing the spade again. He promised to behave, and the spade was yanked from him. He was left on the earth, head in the dust, and the recovery time gave him a minute to calm down.

He gathered himself, tucked in his shirt and beard, and coughed. Then he walked back, away from the sun, back to his whiskey.

A voice behind Harry said, 'See, stranger, that's what I mean about this town needing some

manners. I keep telling folk this. Some little sprinkle of God dust!' This came from Preacher Hoyt, a
man with a smile like a sword-gash and a black suit
pressed so that it could have stood rigid if he
stepped out of it. He was there to meet Lord Harry
and he had recognized him.

'Seen your picture in the periodicals ... Lord
Harry Lacey, I reckon?' Hoyt held out his hand, and
Harry took it keenly. They both managed to smile.

'You'll get used to this kind of thing, Lord Harry
... Sheriff McCoy and Hole are friends really ...
used to be on the same side, and maybe will be
again, I hope.' He saw Harry's look and explained,
as they walked towards the Hoyt home, 'I'm afraid
we live amid ill tempers and trigger-happy sawdust-
heads, Lord Harry. But welcome all the same.
Cherry pie and coffee await you!'

2

At the Big Question, Itch Carney was taking advice
as to whether he should call for the Doc. He was a
man with a rankling, burning purpose in life, which
was to get even with that louse, McCoy. There was
nothing worse, in his opinion, than a partner who
thieves and double-crosses, and that was what
McCoy had done, and even worse, he had been
responsible for a death.

Itch was a big, square man who once in younger
days had done every kind of work a man does on a
cattle trail, including the occasional deviation from
the law in a piece of rustling. Now, however, he had
his steady remuda, good support for food and vet-
erinary work, and everything a man of sixty could
want, if we except the company of a woman. Truth
is, that was nagging at him every day now, since he
planned what was to be his last drive north before
he hung up his ropes and chaps.

Now, that last drive, he had sworn to himself,

could not happen until McCoy was laid low. The only turmoil in his mind right at that time wasn't if he would kill the man, but how and when. Trouble was, Itch was not a well man. Will Ringo, his closest compadre and the nearest thing he had to a son, said that he was sick because his mind was so bent on getting even, but there was something physical, he was thinking.

Itch was basically seen in Broken Man as the big bald hombre with the irritating voice. He had been boss for a long, long time and had the voice to prove it. But this day, when his heart was pumping loud and his legs were wobbly, he was concerned.

Itch sat on an old barrel, watching Will Ringo mend a fence.

'Will, you noticed lately that you're slender as a girl's wrist?'

'Pardon, Mr Itch?'

'I was just thinkin' while watchin' you with that hammer, how slight you are. You sure you're eatin' right?'

'Yeah. I always did worry my parents, I was so little. You want me to eat more raw meat?' This was one of his jokes. He relished teasing the boss, and Carney sort of liked it. He liked to play, but had darkened into a more serious set of values since losing his kid brother.

'No, forget it. Put down that hammer and come over here, son.'

Will pushed back his hat, wiped off some sweat

15

and sat on a stump. 'Something on your mind, Mr Itch?'

The boss wondered how much to say. Then he just went for it: 'Son, you noticed I been different lately?'

'Nope . . . except that you sit around more.'

'Exactly. That's the point. I'm not feeling too good – and here we are planning that drive up to the snow country. You reckon I should see the Doc?'

Will frowned. 'Well, you're the boss. I can't tell you . . . But I have to say that last time you saw Doc Potworthy the result was real strange. I mean, his advice was just stupid!'

'Yeah. You recall he said there was nothin' wrong with me that a good hour with a loving, pure-hearted woman couldn't put right?'

Will nodded and then laughed. 'Yeah, also with that golden medicine bottle!'

'Yeah . . . did work though . . . for a while.' Itch said, scratching his head. 'Maybe I'll see him tomorrow.'

He left Will to the fence and wandered around, feeling like he was going to spew. But he wanted to keep that quiet so he went inside and sat with the old dog for a while, staring at the unused bottle of Golden Medical Discovery on the table. He had been unable to feel strong enough to risk taking it, bearing in mind that he knew two men who had drunk it and died within six months. His rational mind told him that this was just bad luck, and the

Doc was most likely a sound man, but the nag was there, like a kid tugging at your coat. Anyway, as he was feeling rough as a buffalo hide and downright low, he carried on thinking about how he needed a woman. 'She don't have to be a woman as such,' he thought, 'But a wife.'

Then he saw how stupid that line of thought was, and smiled to himself. He ran through the candidates around Broken Man: the woman at the store was too tedious; the girl at the stables was far too young. There was only really one woman he counted as right, and that was Perdy Candle, at The False Start. She was pure-hearted and that stood out like a bullet-hole in the temple.

Yep, decision: he would see the Doc and get put right, and then maybe have an exploratory conversation with Perdy, just to test the ground. The woman could play the piano, he reflected, and she could surely cook. On top of that, well, there was love, if you could tell where it really was. Hell, he just wanted a female around the place, if only to look at. A woman somehow homed a place. You put a female in a square of dust and insects and she'd home it.

That was why, he thought, McCoy was going to be knocked out by a stranger. There had to be nothing they could pin on Itch Carney when McCoy was found dead as a plank in his own office. No, it was a job for his own man, his resolution man, as he termed him. You want to resolve a situation, you sent for the right man. This was the man who had made most of his stash from bounty hunting and now was keen to go north because there was a whole kin of Mexicans reported to be looking for him.

McCoy had killed his brother, gentle, soft-headed Red Carney. Maybe not with a gun, but with ill treatment. He had arrested young Red over something and nothing, and he had died in the jailhouse. That was down to McCoy, damn him. Now the time had come to pay for that. The resolution man was coming. There were plenty of men around who could take McCoy out of the picture, but they were amateurs. The job needed Joe Dane, one of the very best killers. The reason for that was his total lack of emotion. He pretended everything, lied shamelessly, and took what he wanted whenever he felt like it.

Itch knew that his health was shaky, too. There had been much too long a period of sniping and brawling, name-calling and annoying between Carney and McCoy, and now, his problems with his body mounting up, it was time to end it all and do a little thinking about settling scores.

Meantime, he needed to gather some more stock, a cook and a few more hands, and then it was 'so long, Broken Man!' and off on the drive. Then a new thought struck him: hell, if the woman really could cook, then he wouldn't need no cook. The cook problem had come along because of the rat. Corny Mildew had been competent enough with a pan and a fire, and his stew was tolerable, but his fear of rodents had done for him. He had walked out and gone back to Texas just a week earlier and left the Big Question without a cook. It had been a week or so of beans and sour dough biscuits, and stocks were low. That rat had been a sign of bad luck, he thought, and a woman could turn it all right. There was a magic about the weaker sex, Itch thought, recalling his one true love of years back, who had left him for a gambler: 'You're dull, Henry, dull as cold porridge, and you scratch your backside – now that gets to be too much for a lady. Even the loose women love some culture and style.' The habit of talking to himself was another bad sign, he was sure. He was falling apart, and even that he put down at McCoy's door.

He had put every effort into de-lousing himself that time, after he had picked up the bugs on the trail. But that had been too late. She took off without a word more, and he was destined to be a loner.

'That's gonna change,' he said to himself. But first, he was waiting for his resolution man – Joe Dane.

3

Lydia Santo disliked many things, but mostly it was her name. That was even more troublesome for her image of a lady than the cow on the roof of the Santo sod-house. Strictly, it was only partly a sod-house, because Elias Hole, who had adopted her, being a man with a creative turn of mind, had purloined some wood from somewhere, so the place was half sod and half boards.

Her pa had been a rascal called Rico Santo and she was stuck with his name. Now, for the girl, Santo was an undesirable word for obvious reasons, and Lydia, though packed with irony, being a classy name, given that all the Santos had worked as thieves in the past, she hated it because it just sounded bad. It had no style, and style was what she worked hard to achieve. In fact, it sounded plain religious – like *saint* – and that was unacceptable. Hence she repeatedly told the world to call her Liza, for that had class, and it was a word that defined what she wanted to be. One day, she said, time and again, she would be Liza Di Buco, which she had found out in some ladies' periodical was an aristocratic name. In her journal, in which she kept her Liza di Buco thoughts, she wrote it real big: Liza di Buco. That was the name of a STAR.

In *The Journal of Liza di Buco, Actress*, Lydia wrote:

Both Bonneville men stride through the town as if they are part of some royal family. R.W.P. takes careful, studied paces, and the son matches him, by his side. Both look to their front, proudly, and both greet any townsfolk who pass with a polite 'Good day, sir' or 'Good day, madam.' In Broken Man they stand out like a canker on a cow's nose. I shall one day walk with them, or at least, with him, for he is destined to be my partner in life, and I will have no other. It is in the stars that a true love appears to a lady of quality, and the lady always knows. I have to find a way to tell him our destiny.

Writing the journal and dreaming about the made-up Bonneville was one of her little treats of her day, because for the most part in her waking hours she was washing, feeding, slapping, yelling at and restraining the rabble – the gaggle of young Santos that packed the sod-house from corner to rafter. She was supposed to have big brother Winfield to

21

help her and Ma Lil, but he was almost always away learning cow punching and wrangling with Boss Itch. The result was a life of sheer misery and sweat-work for Ma Lil and Lydia. Any time of day there was one of the rabble screaming or destroying some household item. Lydia could only steal away and go out if Ma Lil let her, and luckily, her mother understood about the lusts of the young. In fact, she had been at its mercy so much that her family was in double figures, somewhere around eleven 'if you count strays' she would say when asked.

Lydia spent the hours when the rabble slept, and when she was still awake, looking in her little mirror and practising actressy gestures and pouts. Then she would read her monologues and poems, ready for the day when she had a chance to shine on stage. She would walk around ten paces, turn, and say, 'Good day Sir, my name is Liza di Buco and I'm a theatrical personality. Do kiss my hand.'

She also drew, and she drew Ben Bonneville in various poses, in between the sentences in her journal: sometimes he sat with legs crossed; then he stood and put a finger to his chin, musing; or sometimes she had him walking with a sense of purpose. Then she drew herself: the journal showed the world a small, slender young woman in her early twenties, with long black hair, a sweet, shapely body with good hips and a bosom just forming in a way to attract men's gaze. Best, she knew, were her lips and her smile. She had seen older men fix their stare on her luscious lips or melt as they were enslaved by her smile – and of course these notes went into her journal.

Once Lydia said to Ma Lil, 'Am I beautiful or simply pretty?'

Lil, who was now a rounded, stiff-backed woman of forty, said, 'You will capture hearts.'

Lydia took that as a sort of motto to live by, something that led her forward. But there was just one heart she longed to capture, and that was a challenge, about as tough as riding a bull for more than three seconds, she reckoned. Still, she said sentences like 'Mr and Mrs Bonneville seen here entering the theatre for the performance of Shakespeare. . . .'

Then she giggled and thought how wonderful life could be when there was no angry little face to be wiped or no stink to be removed from a small person's nethers. Sometimes she spoke of herself in the third person and giggled again: 'Liza di Buco, the actress, wipes turds from the ass of a child.'

But somewhere there was a Bonneville.

4

'I was shown how to scalp a man when I was just learnin' to put a second foot out in front and stagger on the ground. . . . Now if that is not a true piece of interesting fact then speak and be honest. My father told me I was born with a scowl, that my first words were *kill the white man.* Yes, I was brought into a world of killing. But this time I was recalling, was when the buffalo trod on my foot.'

Alby Groot took his grubby hands off his belly to stick them in the air and shout in frustration: 'Beg pardon, Mr Two Winds Sir, but can't we shut up that damned pianer?'

'Yeah, the lawyer has a point. We can't have a meeting with that ruckus going on,' Hal Bornless said. Then the strongest, most strident voice spoke over them both. It was Mrs Hoyt, whose words could quell a simmering gunfight. 'Quit moaning and griping. Our society will go on, with or without noise. Now, the subject is the programme of speakers for this new year. It's September – the new year for us, like we had last year, in spite of your strange behaviour, Mr Bornless, and our first speaker is on his way here right now. My good husband is waiting to greet him as we speak.'

Hal Bornless was the man who looked the most alert and alive. He was attached to a red shirt and ill-fitting pants, along with what he called his entertaining boots, complete with silver spurs, and never wore anything else, which is why he sat well detached from the other club members. 'No ma'am, not yet, Mr Two Winds ain't done with his story yet. Anyhow, my behaviour is always strange, Mrs Hoyt, it's my profession. Jests and japes, belly laughs and ballads y'see.'

'Back to business, back to business, ignore the music next door. You were saying, Mr Two Winds?' This was Doc Potworthy, who thought of himself as secretary and leading light, next to Mrs Hoyt of course.

'We can leave my story till next time. The lady is right. We should talk about the programme.' Chet chewed a cigar and then belched. He was a mass of muscle gone a little spacious, but no one dared say he was fat. 'It's a good time for me to remind every-body just why we started up this group. We determined, if you folks recall, to offer the good cit-izens of Broken Man some recreational options beyond shootin' at rats and brawlin' in the back alleys.'

'Mr Two Winds,' Preacher Hoyt responded, 'You

really should have gone in for writin' these here novels. Your brain manufactures supposed facts quicker nor a rabbit escapin' a hawk. You ever thought of writin' down your lies?'

'Lies? By God sir, everythin' I say is grounded in truth!'

'Now calm it down you two, or the cultured folks is like to have a duel on its hands!' Hal Bornless said.

Alby Groot, who was many things, picked up the notion of a duel. One role he played was as undertaker and coffin-maker in the town, and he made his point, 'If the world went back to the sheer wildness of your youth, Chet, I'd be a rich man. They would be deaths comin' at me from all sides and I'd be generatin' cash enough to buy a mansion.'

'Just cut out the gripin' and whinin', Alby, and remember that you're here to advance the cause of poetry and fine conversation.' This was Mrs Hoyt.

Everyone was then mumbling or insisting on a break for a drink, but the Doc took over, putting on his official voice, the one he used when he was selling his *Golden Medical Discovery* and patent puniness curative for little ones. 'Now, if we're movin' on to activities and such, well, I have a guest speaker in mind.' He smiled, as if there was a deep secret about to be revealed and he was the only one privy to the information.

'You're like a man with two legs sittin' with maimed war veterans, Doc, get on with it,' Alby said, in between nibbling a chunk of bread and fat.

Mrs Hoyt frowned. 'Look everyone, I must be serious for a moment and call for order. This town is riven apart by hatred. McCoy and Carney simmer with such murderous savagery that soon we'll all suffer from their bloodthirsty intentions . . . and it's up to our Society to bring in some much-needed culture to this town.'

Doc Potworthy beamed even wider and then announced, 'Quite right, good people. Broken Man is entirely typical of the new communities being set up out West, and someone needs to show that civilization has reached these parts. The West is not all about bullets and daggers. This is why I have arranged for this guest from back East, a real man of letters, a celebrated name in the publications of such homes of culture as Boston and St Louis . . . in fact, he is a man of British blue blood!'

'By God, he's covered some dust then! He desperate for employment?' Alby asked.

The Doc was a hairy man, everywhere except on his head, which was bald as a weathered rock, and his facial hair was well inside his mouth, so that he puffed out strands of grey hair every time he spoke, and his tongue lashed out onto his lips. 'Trust a lawyer to be all critical and little-brained! Nope, he's a speaker of some note, his political and literary talks reported in respected journals from every corner of the land – even in Texas I'm told.'

'Doctor, surely no one in Texas reads? The very

idea is ludicrous!' Mrs Hoyt chuckled.

'Beg pardon ma'am, but my Ma was from Texas and she read news sheets every week, even without talking the reports out loud!' the Doc said.

They all stared at him, unimpressed, so he shut up and muttered something obscene. Mrs Hoyt thought that a family that tolerated red jackets were beyond all estimation and were best shunned.

'Will you listen?' The Doc shouted this so loudly that the piano music stopped and the boozers in The False Start saloon stopped for a few seconds, expected gun shots from the back room, but then went on, most with their eyes on Perdy Candle's stretch of bare leg, seen as she sat at the piano, singing sweetly of old-world romance.

'This man is willing to come here for two hundred bucks,' said the Doc, looking smug.

'Well course, I'd go cause a belly laugh in Rapid City, South Dakota for two hundred!' Hal Bornless said. The others all nodded and made approving noises.

'Right, well if you're all gonna be brutes and jaw-boned Calibans, then I'm going to do something useful like tend a broken limb! I knows when I am not appreciated for what I am – a man of learnin'.' The Doc was ready to sulk.

As he stood up, Mrs Hoyt saw that her little group was in danger of being reduced, so she appeased him. 'Dear Doc Potworthy, do sit down again, and have some of this sarsaparilla, yes? Then we'll all say what a wonderful speaker your man will be.'

They all agreed, except for Hal, who was still worried about the competition, as he saw himself as the primary laugh inducer around Broken Man. He aspired to be the comic maestro of the Colorado Territory, and he made sure all his friends knew that. 'Now, yes, this is a fine idea, but Doc, is this man a serious type? Does he have great themes, noble rhetoric?'

'Oh yes, he's a man of classical learning. Very serious, very proper.' The Doc smiled again, feeling welcome. Hal was happy. The man sounded like a dull bore of the highest degree and was no rival in the comedic art arena.

'Then, it's resolved, that we shall have a collection to pay for this man to come.' Mrs Hoyt said, adding, 'Where is he coming from?'

'Oh back East. . . . I don't know. I think somewhere in Nebraska.' The Doc had no idea. He had simply read about this man in a newspaper.

'His name?' Mrs Hoyt asked.

'Oh, he's called Lord Harry Lacey.'

There was an immediate and deep silence. Then Mrs Hoyt spoke, in a tone of whispered amazement and reverence. 'Did you say "Lord?" '

'Yeah, a lord, from England.' Doc now laughed with glee.

'A lord, and he's only asking two hundred bucks?' Hal asked.

Only Chet Two Winds was unmoved. He lifted a

layer of old muscle off the table, ready to stand up, and said, 'Lords are nothing to sing about. I skinned one once, in Montana, after I stuck him with an arrow through his throat. He died slow.'

The literary folk of Broken Man stared in silence, unable to find any words to give Two Winds that would add any comfort to the subject. But everything came to a halt as Lord Harry walked in, alongside Hoyt, who announced the arrival of their guest as if they were dealing with royalty. Harry was almost mobbed, so enthusiastic was the reception. Then he was sat down at the end of their long table and questions were fired at him. Where had he come from? Had he met Queen Victoria? Did he take part in the Charge of the Light Brigade?

Finally, Mrs Hoyt called for quiet and explained that their guest was weary and also very hungry. She had arranged for coffee and pie, and some cold meats, and these were being brought in by Happen Boodle and his hotel staff. Word had spread around the saloon and the rooms above that a British lord was in town, and the good inhabitants of Broken Man came to stare through every available doorway or window.

Harry was not allowed to go to his bed until he had sung two or three patriotic or romantic songs. Eventually off he went, too exhausted even to undress.

5

There might have been fun and games in the saloon and in the club room, but over at Carney's place there was serious talk. Joe Dane had been fed and watered too, but now he was sitting with Itch Carney and Will Ringo at The Big Question. They were sharing Carney's best whiskey, sitting around the table in the work-room where Carney had most privacy, and the Boss was explaining the job in hand.

'See, Joe, we know each other pretty well, right? You know the situation.'

'Sure do. The lawman done you wrong, so he has to leave the card-table and walk out of the saloon for keeps. The cemetery awaits . . . if this excuse for a town has one yet!' Joe Dane liked smiling. He was always proud to say he hadn't a serious bone in his body, and he would chuckle.

'You cheer me up, young Joe. I wish I had a son like you!' Itch slapped the man on the back and nodded for Will to bring more whiskey.

'Joe, I'd like you to keep in mind the solid fact that McCoy killed my brother Red . . . my little kid brother.'

'Bastard!'

'Yeah, keep that in your mind when you have him close and you've cocked your revolver, son. You savvy?'

'Sure. Now Mr Carney sir . . . if it's not too painful . . . how did your brother die?'

'Joe, he died in the worst way. Alone, in a cell, nobody listenin' to his cries for help. You register that? That's the kind of animal we're dealing with, and he calls himself the representative of the law. Since that suspicious death, we've walked wide of each other, but if his friends meet my friends, there's spite and there's digs and sometimes there's fists. You see the situation?'

'Yes, Mister Carney. I seen these things afore. T'all comes of the basic cowardice of not bein' able to close the show. Everythin' gits a little edgy. Tempers fray, remarks are made. Your boys spit on his boys, and then one day, boom! There's deaths and sufferin' beyond the bounds of the real issue. Yep, I seen it afore.'

Joe Dane stood up and walked across to the window. He saw a melancholy dusk settling on the open plain, and all he could hear was the lowing and complaining of the steers, with a few shouts from the hands. He let some silence settle for a while, before turning around and looking Carney straight in the eyes. 'Mr Carney, there's the law, and there's the law of the gun. I got the latter. There's the law of the state, and there's my law. I got the latter. See, justice tends to step in to help the strong ones, am I right?' He smiled, and the broad smile broke into a laugh.

Carney liked it. He held out a glass of whiskey. 'Will, I like this young feller . . . he's my type. Now, I have a proposition above and beyond this little job of removing the bastard McCoy from his life . . . Joe, how about you take over the star round here? The McCoy brothers been tradin' like this for years. Course, two of 'em is now dead as last year's corn, but for a while they worked the system to suit themselves. We could do the same. You'll be my lawman and I'll make sure you have an easy time. Shake on it?'

Dane was stone-faced now. He was thinking it over. 'Mr Carney, it would be an honour! You do know that I'm here for another reason, not just for your job? I'm here to propose marriage. Yep, my first girl . . . I've come back for her . . . Lydia Santo!'

The others wished him good luck and raised their glasses again. 'I figured it was time I put down some roots. She's always been my girl, Carney, you know that.'

'Sure. You mentioned her in your letter. Good luck son. But I can't see you leaving your trade for good. Hard to see a married man living by his gun, Joe.'

'No. You're right. The resolution man will hang up his holster . . . McCoy is the last job, sir!'

Will Ringo, being young and impressionable, had been dying to ask a question of the newcomer. 'Joe . . . how many have you done away with . . . you and that there Colt?'

'How many times have I been asked that question! Will, I can tell you that Sheriff McCoy will be the nineteenth victim.'

'The nineteenth victim! I like that. I like that a lot . . . you know, I'm gonna scrawl them words on his tombstone, what do you say, Boss?'

Itch Carney and Joe Dane were laughing again. 'The nineteenth victim . . . Sheriff Bastard McCoy . . . I love it, Will my boy, I love it!' There was so much noise that Carney's two great dogs came in to join the frolic. They were beasts that could have hunted wolves, and he loved them better than anything else on his land.

He fussed them and slapped them playfully, saying to anyone who would listen, 'You know, my boys, when we've done this, I'll have to give this God-forsaken wasteland another name . . . maybe Carneyville, eh?' They laughed again, clinked glasses, and the dogs howled.

As for Harry, he was tired but found it hard to sleep. The literary folk had arranged accommodation in a room at Mrs Hoyt's place, at the end of a street that seemed at first to have a degree of peace and quiet

– but sometime after midnight he was awake and nervous, as outside there was trouble. He heard a familiar name being called: Hole.

He rubbed his eyes and went to the window. There below was the sheriff again, and a few yards from him and holding a dagger in a threatening way, was Elias Hole.

'Now Elias, we had a run-in over that damned hound. You should be home with the family. I don't want to have to arrest you man, because they need you.'

Elias was swaying, clearly the worse for drink, and this became obvious as he spoke. 'See Mr Lawman, I know this town thinks I'm crazy. Yes, they do, right? So, yes, I know I have my little ways. Maybe strange little ways, but I don't do no harm unless I'm provoked, and you know what, McCoy? You provoke me.'

'Elias, sure you have some odd ways. What with your booze and your tempers and the damned animals you collect . . . I mean, that's strange. But deep down you're a good father, and I don't want to see you mixed up with Carney's boys. I want you on the side of law.'

A crowd began to gather. Windows opened and shouts bellowed out, demanding that peace and quiet were required. The good folk of Broken Man went out on to the street and stood behind their sheriff. 'Lock him up, McCoy,' one voice prompted. Another said, 'He's loco. He's a danger to the community, McCoy.'

For a moment there was a static stand-off, with nobody doing anything. Then this was broken by the shriek of a woman's voice, and from somewhere there came Lydia Santo, and she went to Elias and wrapped her arms around him, ignoring the danger of the knife.

'Pa, come home! I need you, and we all need you . . . come home!'

Sheriff McCoy wanted to let him go with her, but the pressure of the crowd weighed heavy and he needed to push his authority.

'Elias, I'm sorry but I'll have to take you in. You wounded a man back in the bar. There were plenty of witnesses. Come over here and be a good man, let the law take its course.'

'Sure . . . so I can die in your jail. That's what happens when the law takes its course!' McCoy nodded to a man who had arrived and who stood with the crowd. This was a command for the man and several others to rush Elias, as he had his arm around Lydia. They came at him, one pushing the woman away, and the other grabbed their man and forced him into the dust. He was sat on and hand-cuffed. The crowd applauded and gradually dispersed.

'Justice ought to operate on a one-to-one mindset, McCoy. It didn't ought to gang up on a fellow!' Elias whined.

Harry saw McCoy being patted on the back, being told that was good work. But as he was led away, Elias shouted his threat. 'Carney's going to see to this, you wait and see. I'm his man, and he'll stand by me ... you cheap excuse for a lawman. Your days are numbered, McCoy!'

Everyone walked off, except for the sheriff, who stood and looked around, seeming to be thinking about the threat. Then his eyes caught the curtain of Harry's room being moved and he looked up. McCoy gave a wry smile, dusted off his hat against his trousers, and turned around, following his prisoner.

6

Happen Boodle was stuck with his name because
nobody could pronounce his real name, which was
so German that it had presented insuperable diffi-
culties to the locals when he first settled in Broken
Man six years back, as he brought his considerable
business acumen to the development of the frontier
town. He and his friends Doc Potworthy and Hal
Bornless had allied themselves with Hoyt and the
churchmen for common benefits as they dug in
some civilization where there had previously been
only sagebrush and dirt with some ramshackle
wooden huts strung along the track.

Boodle had become the cornerstone of civilized
life; he had tried hard to introduce something more
than card tables and dancing girls showing bare
legs. He had quartets and tenors, comedians and
actors, and any number of entertainers booked to
come out to Colorado over the years, and the literary club supported everything he organized. He

and Perdy were known and valued by everyone in town, though he had his eccentricities, and came to expect a little teasing from time to time.

On the morning after the altercation with Elias Hole and the mad dog, he had been reassured by the arrival of the cultured visitor from back East and was doing his best to gather support for the speech that evening in his best back room, where special dances and theatricals were usually presented. By mid-day he and Perdy Candle were sitting by the long bar, planning ways of ensuring there was a good crowd for the English lord.

'He really an aristocrat, Happen?' Perdy asked, with her usual tone of dubious implication.

'Perdita my darlin', you have to know the man's credentials. He's a son of Lord Kelpie, who, I am reliably informed, owns the county of Norfolk – a big place by British standards, about the size of Rackwell County across the river.'

Perdy was 'Perdita' whenever Happen was feeling comfortable and easy with life, and that was not too often these days. He was solid and square, with oil-flattened dark hair and a double chin below his elbow-moustache. The German accent was still there, and he always looked for opportunities to talk about Vienna, where he had been born forty odd years back. He had enjoyed several fortieth birthdays, and only Perdy, who was like a little sister to him, knew his real age. She was slim, elegant and blonde: every inch a lady, all the locals agreed, and

39

lately she had been the subject of universal gossip regarding Henry Carney. 'Itch is wanting her for a wife' had been whispered in a dozen conversations, all overheard by Perdy as she poured beer and whisky at the bar.

'Now, Perdita my darlin', I want you to put one of these here sheets of quality paper into every hand that holds out a dollar to you today, right?'

She looked at it and then read out the words, ' "Lord Harry Lacey will speak on law and justice. He is a legal expert with qualifications from England's most esteemed university of Oxford." Impressive, Happen. You must be on your best behaviour. No panics . . . no bad moods. Keep the mad-stone in the drawer.'

'My mad-stone has settled more drunken arguments than any pistol. I can knock a man flat out with it, quicker than you can say hallelujah.'

'Fine. I'll tell every customer how wonderful the Lord is. Though in my experience a man lies as naturally as he sinks whiskey. It just comes natural like. That's why I'm still not hitched to any man's wagon in this life . . . not even yours, Happen. How many times have I turned you down, my love?'

'Four. I'm not trying again. I know when I'm beat.'

At that moment, the doors swung open and most of the town literary society walked in, with a very tall man in the midst of their gaggle of noise. This was Lord Harry, and his fair hair, now washed and combed, made him look more distinguished than he had as the stage passenger. Perdy picked him out right away. 'Well, this must be the man!' she said, standing up and with her arms akimbo, looking right at him, as he was introduced by Doc Potworthy. 'Mr Boodle ... Miss Candle ... may I introduce our speaker for this evening, Lord Harry Lacey.'

Happen stepped forward and shook Harry's hand. He had to look a long way up so he could speak face-to-face, and then Perdy did the same. She gave a curtsey.

'Lord Harry ... real pleasure, my Lord ... could I ask, are you related to the Queen of England?'

'Way back in the family tree, I guess. My father always said so! But who cares about that?'

'Please everyone, sit down ... I'll have coffee brought.'

Happen clicked a finger, and then, as his barman ignored him, he clapped his hands loudly and snapped out, 'Coffee for the Lord!' The barman, still with a sore head from the previous night, thought Jesus was in the bar, and had to be told that this was a real English lord, and he and the literary folk needed coffee.

Happen sat Harry at one end of a long table and the literary folk sat around, admiring their guest in his smart dark suit and fancy waistcoat. Mrs Hoyt had dressed up her guest immaculately, and had even provided some eau de cologne.

As coffee arrived, Harry decided to deflect any further talk of himself and asked Happen, 'Mr Boodle, do I detect a German accent?'

'You do sir, and let me tell you that I am from Vienna, the mother of all culture and the fine arts. A little of that will be sprinkled around here tonight, yes? Now you come at a significant moment, my Lord, because I'm hoping that I shall be the first mayor of this town. My friends and I, around this table, have resolved to make Broken Man a place where good folk may walk along the street without fear. It will be a place formed and forged by respect for the law. . . .'

Before he could complete the sentence, there was the sound of a voice yelling out in the street, and the customers in the bar, all weary cowboys and assorted drifters, stood up to a man and scrambled to the door and windows to see what was happening. Someone called out, 'It's Sheriff McCoy . . . one of the Carney boys is resisting arrest!'

The literary club sat firm at first, refusing to show any interest in a street altercation. But then Chet Two Winds stood up and strode to the door, saying, 'Never could resist a scrap!'

Out in the street, McCoy was facing Will Ringo, who was standing over the prostrate body of a man, with his foot on the victim's chest.

'Now, Ringo, come along with me, son. I saw you assault this man. This is a visitor to our town . . . what's he done to offend?'

'What he's done is pick my pocket, you see, Squint, and I hit him maybe a little harder than I meant.'

He lifted his foot away and the man in the dust squirmed and grunted, struggling to his feet. 'Sheriff, I want this man arrested. I never took no cash and he came at me. It was an unprovoked attack.'

'Fine, well, I saw you hit him Will, that's all I can say. Seems we have no witnesses.'

The man was now on his feet, flapping the dirt from his coat. Will said he would let the matter go, as he had the money back, if the sheriff would forget it.

'You can't forget it, lawman. You're to do your job and arrest this scum!' The stranger snapped, stepping towards the sheriff and prodding his chest with a finger.

McCoy didn't like that at all. 'Sir, till you started irritating the hell out of me, I was going to take your word for it, but now, well you can just move on. I got some coffee going cold in my office.' He strode away, leaving Will Ringo smiling at the stranger. The smile became a laugh, something full of ridicule. The stranger walked away, back towards the stables. Then, just as the audience in the saloon were about to return to their drinking and cards, the stranger turned and shouted again. The crowd surged to their places by the window and the door.

At that moment Lydia, who had been shopping

for her pa, Elias, walked out of the store, carrying a heavy basket of provisions, going towards the stranger, and this was just as he fired at Will Ringo. The bullet whistled past Will's head, and Will turned, aimed and fired. The stranger dived for cover, and the bullet hit Lydia in her arm. With a squeal of pain, she fell down, her basket spraying its contents across the street.

There was a dark silence, in which all eyes turned to the girl, lying on the boards by the stables. Someone called, 'The girl's been shot!' and in a matter of seconds, Harry was on his feet and racing outside shouting out 'Where is she?'

He soon found her and saw the wound. The bullet had gone through her upper arm. She was whimpering but holding an expression of toughness on her face. The blood had seeped into a shirt she wore, and Harry saw that a tourniquet was needed. His bandana was soon tight around the wound. 'You'll be fine, miss . . . just lie still. Help is coming.'

'My Pa . . . he's in jail over there. I was taking him some bread.'

'Never mind him, miss. Try to take it real easy now.' His broad, firm hand lay on her forehead and then she felt it move and go to the pulse at her wrist. His soothing words continued. Then the crowd arrived, and Harry had to urge them to stand back, out of the way.

Doc Potworthy was finally at the scene and he

took over. Lydia gave Harry a smile before she was lifted and taken inside the nearest store, where there was no crowd and little noise.

Harry stayed by the door, watching and listening. It was some time before the literary club gathered again, without the Doc, and as they sat again in The False Start, the talk was all about the trouble.

'It goes on, this stupid war. Now we have a casualty who leans neither way!' Hal said.

Mrs Hoyt tutted and moaned, then said, 'I can't see how it's ever going to end, except in a few deaths!'

Chet Two Winds, always abrupt and direct, turned to Harry and asked, 'Lord Harry, you're talking about justice tonight. How does it apply here, sir?'

I wish I knew he said to himself. Then he spoke, 'All I know is, guns and fists don't resolve anything. They just make for more killing.'

The Doc came into the saloon, managing a smile. 'She's gonna be all right. *This* time, anyway! But who's able to stop these Carney men? The bad blood between Carney and McCoy is likely to ruin this town unless somebody does something!'

Hal Bornless had a reply: 'Let's face it, folks, the law stops at Bedford County . . . two hundred miles east!'

7

Squint McCoy had retreated to his office. The shooting had been only one more in a tiresome list of daily violent incidents. The only problem was that it was one of Carney's boys who had fired the shot. It was an accident, that's all, and some bystander had been hurt, but he wasn't clear about who that was. Elias Hole, now virtually sober again, was hammering against the jail wall with his massive fists and the cell was shaking. Then there was Aby Silvera, the Mexie, a man who knew the inside of the Broken Man jailhouse better than his own chin, which was usually smeared with blood from his latest fracas with the locals.

It had always been a tight, manageable, toe-the-line kind of town, barely earning the right to be placed on a map. But that was fine: he dreaded the thought of any expansion. At the current size, a man could watch every movement, from a new arrival in town to the good lady who put her nose

46

into everyone's business, shaking out a rug outside her domain. That was Alby Groot's wife, and she kept well out of things since he gave her a scare. That was the secret: let the boys do some frightening in the case of anything that stood in the way of the McCoy empire.

For McCoy, the law was there to preserve the peace – his peace. As for the general peace of his patch of Colorado, well that could wait indefinitely. If he could wipe out the Carney lot, the whole damned tribe, he might just win some feet-up drinking and thinking time, undisturbed by knife work and gun shots.

But on this particular day, he was about to be under siege. The townsfolk were more than tolerant when drifters and criminals were casualties of street fights, but now a young woman lay in Doc Potworthy's surgery with a bullet hole in her arm. That was unacceptable, and the members of the literary club complained so loudly and noisily that Chet Two Winds decided to act.

Now, the whole extent of Broken Man, from hotels to sod houses, knew that Chet was all talk, a rambling, unreliable tale-teller, but his one use was in leading some kind of riot – so no sooner had he shouted, 'To the sheriff!' than a crowd of restless types, drunks and riff-raff gathered and stuck to him like burrs to a steer's backside. Soon around sixty rowdies were standing outside the sheriff's office, and Chet was given a wooden crate to stand on, so he could be seen by all as he gave his speech and spoke for them all, after such an outrage.

Just as Elias Hole had discovered that a tin cup smashed against iron bars could make a sound enough to wake the dead, Chet began his harangue.

'Now see, Squint McCoy, we're here, your own folk, the people you're paid to protect, and a short while back, one of us – a young woman called Lydia Santo – was gunned down in plain daylight. Where is the culprit? He's back at Itch Carney's ranch scoffing pie and soaking up whiskey. Yep, he's Will Ringo, and he's scum. Where should he be? Why, in your jail, waitin' for the judge to order a spell behind bars. Come on out, you spineless excuse for a man . . . come out and explain yourself!'

McCoy realized that the girl was Hole's girl, and he seized the moment to take advantage. His deputies were all out in a posse searching for some renegade with a rifle and no morality, bent on making hell settle in Colorado. The answer for now was Elias, who was sober and full of hatred for Carney, who had fired him twice and refused to give him a good name with anyone else, seeming to be content to see the entire Hole family starve.

'Elias, you want to be a deputy?'

'You serious, McCoy? With pay and such?'

'A trainee first. Probationary period of one month. Two bucks a day and chow. I mean, you're usually on the wrong side of the law, but the truth is, I'd prefer a man like you to be on my side . . . you see my thinking?'

'I do, boss, I sure do. You're serious? I mean, you would give me a star?'

'You know, Elias, I always believed that a man painted bad is misunderstood. Give a rebel some discipline and some responsibility, why that man can turn to do good, just feelin' important. I think it's your turn to be tested, Elias.'

'You mean, I could be Deputy Elias Hole, of Broken Man . . . instead of the town nuisance? Why, my family's gonna think some spirit had slipped into their pappy and taken over. . . .'

'One condition. You help me disperse this crowd out there and you help me rub out the Carney boys.'

'It'll be a pleasure. Open the damned cage, boss!'

Elias was freed, and his huge frame now had a deputy's star pinned on, at the most solid part of his broad chest. McCoy led him out and they faced the crowd.

Chet saw this unlikely sight and guffawed so loudly that the box beneath him almost gave way. 'So, sheriff, you're so desperate that you're employing drunks and brawlers!' The crowd jeered.

McCoy waved his arms for quiet and eventually he got it. 'Folks, this is my new deputy and you will respect him. Now I sympathize with the young girl, and I'm sure that Mr Hole, her adopted Pa, will want to see her. . . .'

Elias' face suddenly went a deep red as he realized what had been said. 'You mean, my Lydia . . .

49

she's been shot?'

'Afraid so, but she's fine . . . with the Doc,' Chet said.

Elias was soon running down the street, sweating and panting, determined to see how his girl was doing.

In fact, she was doing well, and Harry had been sitting with her. The Doc had given her all the treatment she needed, and she was bandaged and quiet. She had even tolerated his special golden medicine to please him. Now she lay still, looking into the face of Harry Lacey, and thinking she saw her Bonneville.

'Did you save my life, mister?'

'No. The bleeding was not so bad that you would have died, but we have to be sure.'

Harry held her hand at first, and then gave her a few sips of brandy.

'Mister, is it true that you're an English Lord?'

'Sure. Lord Harry Lacey, at your service. I think you're Lydia Santo, right?'

'Well, not for long. See, I'm going to be a singer and an actress. I'm going to be Liza di Buco, the entertainer. That's the plan, sir.'

'Call me Harry.'

She didn't tell him, but as she looked at him, again she could see her Bonneville. An aristocrat, holding her hand, in Broken Man, Colorado! Was this all a dream? The words were running through her mind already – the words that would be in her journal: *Liza di Buco, gunned down in the wild border town, found herself looking up into the brooding face of an English aristocrat, a man who was notably above the barbaric denizens of the town where nobody was safe after dark, and where a woman's lot was sheer drudgery from dawn till dusk. . . .*

She felt light-headed and sleep took over. Harry stroked her long hair from her face and left her to rest.

'You have children, my Lord?' asked Doc Potworthy, who was standing near, checking the patient was doing well. Lydia was shaken from her dreaming, and listened to every word her new hero uttered.

'No, sir. Please call me Harry.'

'Sure. Now, you did well today. You seem to have some medical know-how, Harry.'

'Some. I seen some people dead and some just missin' death's clutches.'

'Well, I reckon you might have saved her young life, my friend.'

'Yeah. It's all one big balance sheet, I think . . . after all, I *took* a few.'

He walked out, a wry smile on his face as he saw the Doc take in that last assertion. Harry couldn't know it, but for the rest of that day, the Doc was chewing over that remark. At around seven, when he was dressing ready to attend Harry's talk, with his wife, he had the thought running through his head that their genteel English speaker had been a killer of some kind. As the literary club gathered and sipped their sherry, waiting for Harry to arrive, he whispered to Hal Bornless and to Hoyt, 'You know, there's more to Lord Harry Lacey than meets the eye.'

'What are you saying, Doc?' Preacher Hoyt asked, puzzled.

'I think he's more than the surface lets you think, that's all I'm saying.'

Word went around. Gossip and rumour ran through Broken Man's more cultured citizens as they took their seats in the special entertainment back room of The False Start. By the time this talk had percolated around the place, the general opinion was that their guest was a bounty hunter or a robber, and the man in the stage, who had suspected this from the beginning, persuaded everyone that the speaker was a killer, here in disguise. That escalated again, so that folk started speculating about who he was in town to murder.

Strangers to the town were ordinarily ignored. They were fine as long as they paid for their drinks, kept their guns in their holsters and avoided robbing the locals. But every so often one of this constant train of wanderers stood out and attracted everyone's glances and enquiries. Such a one was Lord Harry Lacey. The man who was at first a drifting killer was soon something far more, once it was observed that he dressed well, washed frequently, spoke civilly and took his hat off when he walked past a lady. After some hours of this kind of behaviour, rumour made him an aspiring politician; then he became the owner of a new silver mine up the valley; some discussed his name and felt sure that they had read about Laceys who owned most of San Francisco.

Harry, sitting with Lydia, soon grasped the reality of what was in her mind: she had romantic love in her blood and bones, and he knew that he would have to press down hard on such nonsense. In fact, being admired and adored by women of any age was almost unknown to him. Of course, heads turned to acknowledge his height and his presence, but there it ended. That is, until he determined his new identity. In his past, he had been so deeply coloured by the smells and juices of the wilderness that he seemed tanned with waste-land living, as other men were imbued with oils and lotions. The former Harry Lacey had been something that drifted in like sagebrush, and he could have carried on being wind-swept till he reached the western ocean or lodged somewhere under the shoulder of a mountain.

But Lord Harry Lacey had been cultivated, shaped by his will to live afresh. He had thought back to the educated men of his mother country, back in the heathlands of Norfolk, and he had made himself into a traditional gentleman. His friends had found all this highly amusing, and he had been mercilessly ribbed for his well styled hair and moustache, and his cleaned and ironed attire. But eventually, what had started as exhaustion and disillusion, living on his wits and with barrels and blades, had now become something he was comfortable with – almost as if a double of himself had appeared.

All he had to do now was talk about the new beliefs that had led him to the transformation. That sounded so simple. But the truth was, he was more nervous about facing a well suited and educated audience than he was the six-guns of the men he had faced in order to kill instead of being killed.

8

The real hired killer, Joe Dane, had headed straight from Carney's place to the Hole homestead, a way out of town. There he had been greeted by Ma Lil and the barrel of a Winchester. She was alone with the children, and there was a good stretch of earth between her home and any help. There was a stranger, astride one of the most solid mounts she had ever seen, a big, broad-chested bay.

On his way there from Carney's place, Dane had been thinking over what to say. It wasn't easy. When he had last been here with Lydia, she had been just fifteen and he had eight years on her. It had all been promises and kisses, and Elias had hated the sight of him. Now here he was again, and with marriage in mind. They had talked about that, and she had dreamed of being a wife, but mainly to escape the drudgery of being second Ma to the bunch of children who filled that chaotic home.

'Who are ye, mister?' Ma Lil asked, with the rifle

pointed at Dane's chest.

'Don't you remember me, ma'am? I'm Joe Dane. I was once real welcome under this roof. I growed some, and I lost a lot of weight. But look again . . . you see me?'

She searched through her memory, and then finally she recalled the man. 'Oh hell and old timbers! You're the seducer of our Lydie. By God you are! Now git, or I'll lay you flat and drag you to the cemetery.'

Dane's inner urge was to draw a pistol and rub her out of existence before she could flicker her eyelid. But he wanted the girl, and that needed patience. He was going to have enough dollars from Carney to set up on his own land, and he needed Lydia to be his woman.

Ma Lil had a good view now, as Dane moved out of the sun, and she saw the gun-belt. It was unmistakably an armoury she associated with a chancer, a man who lived by death.

'Joe Dane, well, blow me son, you used to be welcome here, but then, why, you turned the head of a mere child. For a while she could talk of nothin' but you. Smooth talker I guess?'

'When I need to be. But I'm as honest as a silver dollar. I been away, and I changed. I want to settle down, and this is the place I want to settle in. You see ma'am, Lydia is all I been thinking about. My intentions are to marry her. I have nothing improper in mind, believe me. . . .'

The Winchester was still pointed at him, though now he swung a leg to dismount. But Ma Lil was not having him in the house. She fired so that earth shot up and into the man's boot-tops, and he swung his leg up again. Then she fired again and this time, the bay snorted and shot backwards, almost dislodging Joe Dane. 'Now git out and stay away, Dane, you're bad news. Elias will be comin' looking for you, son, and if I was you I'd run like a prairie dog who's seen the hunter!'

For a second, Dane thought about gunning her down, but he restrained himself and turned away, riding off with a last few words, 'I'll be back, ma'am. Count on that!' He had been struggling to maintain the veneer of good manners and affability, but in his heart he was cursing and damning the woman. Who the hell was she, the old whore, to be threatening Joe Dane? He had a plot ready in the graveyard for her, and a bullet with her name on it. *Damned old bitch.* . . . He cursed and damned her. But it was time to get the job done. Jim Squint McCoy had a date with death first, then the old lady could follow.

Harry was sitting now, on a little makeshift stage that was used for comedy acts touring the area or for small musical groups. He had dressed for the part, every inch of him showing the elegance of a man from back East. He had wanted to use his aristocratic background to push into his new career, and he dressed the part, with time taken to wash hair, moustache and beard; the jacket and waistcoat were pressed, and the trousers also; and then there was the jewellery – some gold rings and a special shiny pendant with crossed swords and a Latin motto, which folk always asked about and he answered, with the only Latin he actually knew: *semper fidelis* – always faithful.

They were all sitting in front of him, expecting to hear wisdom, and maybe with heads full of knowledge and questions. They most likely had lines of bookshelves in their homes, and pianos, and paintings. Was he up to it? He did what he always did when he needed strength and confidence: he smiled and covered over the worries eating at him.

Preacher Hoyt was elected to introduce him, and he raised a hand to quieten the hubbub across the hall, before saying, 'Good folk of Broken Man, I thank you for turning out tonight to welcome our very special guest from England, a real true blue blood from back home, Lord Harry Lacey of Norfolk.' He turned to look at Harry as the audience applauded with enthusiasm. 'Now, you know me, good people, and you know that I speak direct and I never digress into homilies and lectures . . . (there were groans at the irony of that) and so I have to tell you simply that Lord Harry is to speak on justice this evening, something dear to our hearts.'

He shook Harry's hand as his speaker walked across to him, and then Hoyt sat down and left

Harry to stand before the locals. He thought of the vicar back home, and how he always started his sermons with a humorous little line or two, and totally thinking on his feet, he said, 'I sincerely hope you all meant to be here tonight, but if you're in the wrong place, do leave now so I won't be hurt!'

They liked it. There was laughter. The faces of the literary club members looked relaxed. He warmed to his real topic for the night.

'Ladies and gentlemen, good people of Colorado ... I know that the notion of justice is something that tends to float around and take on different colours. It's not one constant item, something anyone may define in a slick and easy way. In fact, it runs through your fingers every time you try to understand how it works. But I'd like to try, and first I want to tell you about a young woman, a mere girl, just fourteen years old, the daughter of my best friend back in Illinois. Now, this little girl was unfortunate enough to be in a family that another family felt some hatred for. In fact, she lived in a place when one bunch of kin wanted another bunch of kin out of the world. The rift began when someone was accused of stealing land. Then it all grew, and the hatred ran like poison through the veins of near on a hundred people. One day, this little girl was riding with her brothers when there was an ambush. Good people, I have to tell you that she was shot dead. Three others died that day, but it didn't stop the hatred.'

He paused and looked around. In the silence, the people in the crowd examined Lord Harry's face, which was showing emotion welling up in him. Then he went to the lectern that Hoyt had set in place for him; he put both hands firmly on the edge and leaned forward, so that he could look the front row in the eyes, and he scanned them all as he said, 'Ladies and gentlemen ... I fired the bullet that killed her.'

There was a sudden groan from the mass of people in front of him. A few voices called out words which were unclear. Harry then added, 'I did some time for it. I walked to the law myself. I see her face every day. Since then, good folk of Broken Man, I have never carried a gun. If I am attacked, these two fists will protect me ... nothing more!'

'God bless a sinner!' Preacher Hoyt yelled out, and a chorus of voices imitated him.

'No, no, I wish to say to you, that justice is not the same as retribution. Now I see, since I arrived here, that once again there is hatred in your streets. I have been told that your officers of law do not have your faith and trust. Well, find new ones, make justice sit with fairness, like the court of Solomon, and siphon off the bad blood. It's the only way to cleanse the spite and the despising of man to man. ... Justice lies in the very heart of that affection and understanding that man should have for man ... the affection he felt for the world when he was a child, and innocent before his Maker ...

'Course, I'm not here to give a sermon. I'm here because I know, in my fairly short life, that we all face adversity, and that we overcome that with moral courage, not with a will to destroy the person we perceive as our enemy. Now I hope that all makes sense to you good folk of Broken Man!'

There was a general applause after those words. Preacher Hoyt came out to him and shook his hand. Then he called for quiet and asked for questions. 'Lord Harry will be pleased to answer any questions you have. . . .'

At first there was quiet again, but then a voice from the back called out, 'Lord Harry, would you be surprised to know that we was told you was a killer . . . that under your fancy long coat you got pistols, and that Carney or McCoy is paying you for some evil. What do you say to that?' There was a universal sound of offence and shock. 'Some of us was informed that under that smart suit of clothes, there's a hired gun, waiting for the victim to come along. What do you say to that?'

Alby Groot, who had been keeping out of things since the stranger arrived, thinking that his popularity with the club was on the decline, decided to join in. 'Yes sir . . . could you explain yourself? We are respectable folk here.'

'I say that it's nonsense.' Then Lord Harry Lacey started taking off his long coat, and threw it on the stage floor. The he took off his waistcoat. There was no gunbelt, not around the waist or the shoulders.

He then took off his boots and threw them on the stage. 'No guns hidden in these ... no guns anywhere at all. Just these.' He put up both his fists.

Preacher and Mrs Hoyt, Hal Bornless, Chet Two Winds and Doc Potworthy came on to the stage, shook Harry's hand, and then Hoyt turned to the audience and said, 'Folks, you are looking at the Broken Man Literary Society and we believe that proper moral behaviour and the love of brother for brother and sister for sister will create a civilized West out here, more Boston than Boston, right?'

There was a loud chorus of approval and the entire audience stood up and shouted, 'More Boston than Boston!'

9

When Itch Carney set out for The False Start with Will Ringo and Joe Dane in tow, he had declared a halt in the real business of removing McCoy from his life and in fact, he made ready to play a part in a special night for Happen Boodle and Perdy. They had been partners in the hotel and bar for six years, and it had been announced through the town that a celebration was arranged.

'Now, Joe, I know you're here with a certain task in hand, but let's take a night off. The point is, as Will here well knows, I'm going to ask Perdy for her hand in marriage, and this is the perfect time to do that . . . Right, Will?'

'You been working up to it since the New Year. Plain cowardice, boss!' He laughed, and Carney joined in. They were sitting around, soaking up some whiskey in the big room where Carney kept an arsenal of weapons and a number of hunting trophies. Through his life, he had loved, more than anything, shooting and killing any beast considered wild or food. He had kept mementoes of the best shoots, along with the most testing cattle drives in his life as a cowman. In one corner there was a pile of hides taller than any man he had ever seen, and along one wall was his collection of tribal spears and arrows, leather-work and clothing, all from the Indians on the plains.

Carney was in a nostalgic mood, as he had sunk four large whiskies already, and was standing in the middle of the room now, letting Will adjust his belt and waistcoat, and brush down the back and front of his best jacket. 'Now you boys, you're young, heads hotter than a bushfire, all eager to go and take hold of life like a coyote with a rat. Now a point comes when the struggle has to stop. A man has to shift away all obstacles and get what he wants, then settle down. We got my last drive coming up, and I like to think that before I leave, this place will be all mine . . . all Carney's domain. I like the word domain, eh boys? Sounds like there's power there. A man with a domain, he's respected . . . he's feared. Right?'

They both nodded. Joe Dane said: 'My domain's gonna include Lydia and a stack of dollars, boss.'

Will joined in: 'Mine's gonna be somewhere away from this hell-hole. San Francisco for me, Mr Carney, when I've done working for you.'

Carney took another fill of whiskey and walked across the room to look out over his land. 'Boys, I'm impressed. Young men ought'a have vision, ought to be hungry for something. I like you boys. Now learn from this older man with a desire to shake the sawdust from his brain, and watch him find Mrs Carney this evening . . . see, I have a sprinkle of romance in these bones after all. See what I got here?' He brought from his pocket a small box, which he opened – and there inside was a diamond ring, sparkling so that the boys were dazzled as they closed in to wonder at it.

The younger men couldn't fail to notice that the expression on Carney's face changed. It was as if a dark cloud had passed over his mood. He playfully punched Will on the arm, and then swaggered around a little as if he wanted them to see that he was wrestling with some thought.

'I do have another little line of thought though, boys, under all this talk of letting loose.'

'Well, let's hear it, boss. I can feel some orders coming on. I've learned to know the signs,' Will said.

'Boys, I have the romance, yes. But I have to add a little fact here. Who owns The False Start? Why, Mr Boodle and Miss Perdy. Now, should Mr Boodle happen to meet with an accident and find himself inside a little plot of dust feeding weeds, who would have all his considerable wealth? Yes, Perdy Candle. Now if she had a husband. . . .'

Will and Joe Dane both reacted in the same way – with a gasp of acknowledgement. Then Will slapped his boss on the back and said, 'I knew you was keen on the lady for more sound reasons, Mr Carney. I always liked your style.'

'But first, boss, Mr Boodle has to meet with an accident, I guess?' Dane asked.

'Oh, he will. It's arranged. See, I have a skilled killer in my pay . . . a man called Joe Dane. He can resolve that . . . he's the resolution man, right? I mean, he could arrange for an unfortunate accident to befall Mr Boodle, particularly when there's five hundred bucks in it.'

Dane smiled and took out one of his Remingtons. He wore a leather cartridge belt with two holsters with his two favourite possessions: these Remington .44.40s. He took out a rag from his back pocket and cleaned the barrel. 'Mr Carney, meet the members of my team, my Remingtons. I also have my Loomis shotgun – nice short barrel. The four of us have a sort of rare skill in resolving problems. I can sense that Mr Boodle is kinda vulnerable right now. I can see into the future. . . . He's likely to experience some misfortune. . . .'

Will thought this was real amusing, and he finished his whiskey before laughing so hard his body shook.

Then, putting on his overcoat, Itch Carney ordered them to follow: the party in The False Start was going to have some unexpected guests. As they rode out of the ranch, dusk was just creeping in, and Carney felt the darkness close in, like his own thoughts. He had had this anniversary in mind for a special event for some time, and a shiver of anticipation ran through him as he led the boys out on to the range.

At The False Start, Boodle and Perdy had spent all day making ready for the party. The main bar was cleared in one corner for the hired band, which was going to entertain, with Perdy singing with them, and the girls from upstairs, who had rehearsed their chorus songs and dances. All the big noises of Broken Man had been invited, their seats placed away from the more rowdy element. The gambling was confined to a small back room, and Boodle had asked Sheriff McCoy to have a man at the door to be there if trouble came along. That role fell to Elias Hole, who had been warned to stay sober and have his fists handy. McCoy had all six of his men around the place, inside and out. This was all because Boodle and Perdy wanted a good, happy time for all, and no trouble.

Happen Boodle was, in his mind at least, in Vienna. It was now eight o'clock, and he had asked the band to play a waltz melody just before he stepped on to the stage, and raised a hand: they stopped playing, and all heads turned to him. Waitresses were taking food around, and the first drinks for the evening were free. From the expressions on the faces before him, all was going well, and people were happy.

'Good people of Broken Man, I ask you to welcome, with some noise, my partner, the beautiful Perdita Candle!' She walked up from the bunch of entertainers behind, to the sound of the waltz once more, and bowed. 'Ladies and gents . . . six years my best friend and I have run this place . . . each year we've got a little closer to how we imagined the place would be when we came west, and dreamed about being where we are now . . . six years of, well, I can't say bliss, but I can say excitement, and that's what I always craved!' There were cheers and applause again. ''Course, Mr Boodle here has tried his best to make me into Mrs Boodle, but, well, the fact is, we're too much the same, and I need a stone to sharpen my blade on!'

Boodle gave her a kiss on the cheek and then left her to sing. The band behind played the first bars of Perdy's special song, *It seems my dreams are yours as well.* There was hush in the room, and she sang with the fiddler behind squeezing out every ounce of feeling from the sentimental song – but as she reached the line, '*My heart is waiting for its call to live*', there was the sound of voices at the door. Heads turned, and there was Elias, holding on to Itch Carney's collar. Dane, just behind, was threatening a fight, and Will was holding him back.

Happen Boodle acted quickly. He walked across, whispered something to McCoy, and then all three men were allowed in and ushered to seats by Elias. When Will and Dane saw Carney smile and shake hands with Boodle, they saw the boss for what he truly was: a master of playing the kind of games that politicians played – the ones about lying, and power, and putting on a deception as sweet as sugar water.

Perdy finished the song, and looked across at Carney, and then at Harry, who was across the room by a side door, sitting next to Lydia; her arm was still bandaged, but she was well again, as all could see. 'Now, we want the chairs moved away and the dancing to begin, folks . . . ladies, mark your cards.'

It was when people stood up and took the chairs away that Dane saw Lydia, and he saw her holding Harry's hand. He saw that she had noticed him and he went straight across to her and took her arm, tugging it from Harry's grasp. 'So, here we are again, mister. On the stage, you never said you were coming here to take my girl!'

Lydia, shocked at seeing Dane, was speechless at first, but then she pulled away from Dane. Harry said nothing, keen to avoid trouble. 'You said you'd come back, and I told you no, Joe . . . I told you it was over. I don't want you now. We were in a dream, a fantasy . . . you had no business coming back here!'

'Take it easy, man, there's nothing going on here. I'm helping the girl recover from that wound. Just being helpful and considerate.' Harry spoke directly. It was all so honest that Joe Dane hated it.

'Well, I don't like it, mister. I'd like you to get out

of her life,' Dane said, with a dark threat in his voice.

Harry put an arm around Lydia, and Dane hit out at him, glancing a blow across his cheek. There was no time for Harry to react, as Itch Carney arrived and pulled Dane back, whispering to him, *Don't forget why you're here, boy. . . .*

It didn't take long for Ma Lil and Elias to push in and keep Dane well away from their girl, who was now sobbing, fighting back the mixed emotions of seeing Dane again when she had erased him from her mind. But a while later she was dancing with Harry, and then with other men, and Joe Dane had to watch, with Will, from a distance. As for Itch Carney, he was busy with the main business. He had waited until he saw Perdy leave the main room and head for a smaller room behind, where he knew the other women would be. He loitered by the door until she came out again, and then gently led her into the corridor that led to the back.

'Why, Mr Carney . . . you got something to say?'

He felt his heart thumping so much it was seemingly in his throat, but he found some words. 'Miss Perdy, we've known each other a long time, and we've had some good times . . . dancing and talking and such, and well, I have something to say for sure . . . I think maybe you know what's in my heart, and, well, I'm more than overdue with this, so you see. . . .'

'Itch . . . say what you have to say. The girls are

ready to come out for the show and I'm with 'em. . . .'

'Fine, then I want you to have this.' He brought out the box with the ring and flicked the lid, so she could see the jewel, glinting in the bright lights. 'I'm asking you to be my wife, Perdy.'

She didn't think. Maybe she should have. She merely let the first words blurt out, with no check. 'No . . . No, marrying you is out of the question, Henry!' She pulled herself away, but he grasped hold of her arm.

'Wait . . . wait . . . I've rushed it, my love, I've got it wrong . . . just say you'll think it over.'

She felt the words *my love* resonate inside her, and she didn't know how to react, how to deal with it all. This was Itch Carney, big boned, bald and strong as a bull. This was a man who let hatred burn him up. But then he had almost asked her before, she knew it. His looks had said the same, many times, and not always when he was drunk. Everything he did and said made it clear that he valued her. But she felt nothing.

'Henry . . . I can't. I'm so sorry, but I can't say yes, and I know that diamond could buy a stage and a team of horses! I'm too close to Boodle . . . he's my rock in life!' She pulled away again.

Inside him a fire raged. He wanted to destroy something, to make the whole town crash down to dust. For now, he had to settle for the nearest door, and his punch was so hard it made a crack in the

71

wood. Then he walked out into the dancing again, seeing the joyful faces all around him. His hands formed into fists; he went to the door, shouting for Will and Dane to follow him.

Outside, he took hold of Dane's collar. 'Tonight . . . get rid of Boodle tonight. Then we'll think about the main job. Here's something on account.' He took a roll of dollars from his inside pocket and put them in Dane's hand. 'There's more money than you ever dreamed of coming your way when I see McCoy's body lying there in front of me . . . you hear that, Joe?'

Dane took the roll and assured the boss that it would be done. 'I'm the resolution man, boss, remember?' He turned and went back to the bar, to play a part again, but one that faded into the shadows and would not be noticed.

'Come on Will . . .. Dane, come to the ranch tomorrow, with the right kind of news, you understand me?'

'Sure, boss . . . sure, Mr Carney.' The time had come for action. Dane knew that when trouble really started, it came after a long stretch of resentment and bad blood. Now he could feel it, almost touch it, as it worked its poison in the streets and homes of Broken Man.

10

Strangely, there was a deal of talk about love later that night. First, in the Hole household, where Lydia, very tired but excited after a night of dancing and singing, and of course, romance, was tucked up in bed by Ma Lil, who was still acting as nurse. But sleep was going to be a stranger to the girl until she was all talked out.

'Ma, do you believe in real, genuine love between folk? I mean, something not the same as the kind of arrangements mostly seen around here.'

'What do you mean, my dear? You puzzle me.'

'Well, I'm not a child any more, Ma. I look around. I listen to people, and I know that most folk wed for money, for finding a partner, for a roof over their head . . . but what about love? Where does that fit it?'

'You been reading the storybooks again, Lydia. You got roses and wine in your head, and beaux from back East bring you flowers and poems . . . oh, oh, I see.' No sooner had she mentioned the East than she saw that the thoughts in Lydia's mind were all about Lord Harry Lacey. She pulled up the blankets and kissed the girl on the forehead. 'Now look, Lydia, I ain't your actual mother, but I sure feel like one, and I love you dearly, girl. I don't want you getting torn apart by these dreamy feelings . . . the man in question is ten years older than you!'

'Ah, so you're reading my mind, like you always did, Ma. I'm not too smart in hiding things, right?'

'Right. Now, you see, you've only ever had one man courtin' and that was a skunk, the one around here now, and he's a bad character. He lives on misery, and it's misery of his making, my girl. Now you said you loved him when you were sixteen . . . now you're smitten with a tall gentlemanly type who knows how to dance and who knows some sweet words to say. But men . . . don't trust any one of 'em. I've had two husbands and three lovers, and they all turned out to be cowards or victims. Stay away from marriage, Lydia.'

'But I can't see how it's so wrong. I mean lots of girls marry older men. Truth is, I can't stop thinking of him.'

'Well, I'm still concerned about that wound, my girl, so I want to see you rest. Sleep now, yes? Promise?'

Lydia nodded and Ma Lil left her in peace and darkness, but running through Lydia's mind were pictures of her singing and dancing, and being spoken to by Lord Harry, with both of them dressed as smart as town big-shots. She saw Liza di Buco, wearing a long evening dress costing a hundred dollars, sipping wine and having men bow before her, smiling their affection. Oh yes, Harry – Lord Harry Lacey – was her Bonneville. Could she dare tell him?

The words that would go in the journal ran through her head: *Liza di Buco took the hand of the tall, handsome stranger from England. The word in town was that he was an actual Lord such as England produced, and he won over people by his charm, good grace and his masculine profile. . . .*

But however attractive the man might be, he did not help a girl get to sleep.

Another person unable to sleep in Broken Man was Itch Carney. He was furious. Will told him how red his face was, and how a few pints of whiskey had gone down his throat that night, and it made no difference. Carney ranted at the moon, the four walls and to anything nearby.

'Damn it, Will, how could she turn me down? I had that ring . . . I had my best suit of clothes on, and I had an offer of security. The ladies thirst for it, don't they? I mean security, safety, protection, in this wild country? I mean, any time you like a hundred desperate wild souls could come storming into Broken Man and raise Hell. Am I right?'

Will Ringo nodded and agreed. That was what was required. He knew his boss's moods and his way of seeing the world.

'Damn that sheriff, and damn that Boodle...'
He paused, and then stopped to consider what he
had just said. 'Hey, Will – did I just order Dane to
kill Happen Boodle? I think I did.'

'You did, boss. He's probably dead as a stuck pig
right now. Poor old German heap o' lard. Maybe
got some lead in his craw and some blood filling his
windbag lungs, hey?' Will started to chuckle.

'This is not so funny, Will. I mean, I did do that,
right? I told Dane to kill the man?'

Carney sat down in a deep armchair, startled and
sobered. 'Oh God! There's no going back then. I
done a foolish thing, Will. I mean, Perdy will just
know I did it. She will. Because she told me that he
was the reason she couldn't wed me!'

Will tapped Carney's arm, in a feeble attempt to
console him. 'Boss, you said that it had to be an
accident. Nobody's gonna suspect you!'

Carney seemed to accept that for a minute, but
then he wiped sweat from his face and sighed. Then
he put one of his tough, leathery hands on his chest
and his breathing went heavy and forced. He fell
forward as he tried to stand up, and then he
shouted out, 'Fetch the Doc, Will . . . I'm dying! Get
him *now*, you idiot!'

It was two in the morning now, but Will Ringo
rode hell for leather into town and hammered on
Doc Potworthy's door. He was expecting to find
Carney dead when he got back to the ranch.

76

*

By the time Elias Hole reached home again, he had taken to the bottle. Having to be abstemious all night and wear an ill-fitting suit had been a strain, and as it turned midnight he started on any available bottle of hooch. In fact, it was Happen Boodle who invited him to stay for some drinks, after everyone else had gone to their beds; though there was one other person inside the now locked doors of The False Start, and that was Joe Dane, who had sneaked off out of sight and was waiting in a dressing room used by Perdy until it was quiet. When he was sure everyone was asleep, he crept out and walked along the landing. From there, in the half light, he could see and hear Boodle and Hole, the latter now decidedly inebriated.

'You know, Mr Boodle, you ain't such a bad sort. At one time I thought you was no more a man than a yelpin' cur, kicked about by the lowest drover. But you surprised me. I mean, you run this place real professional like, and let's be honest, mister, you got Perdy to warm your bed, eh?' With his last words he reached across the table at which they both sat, pushing back their chairs, and slapped Boodle on the arm.

'Now I have to tell you that you're wrong, Mr Hole. The lady and myself are simply business partners.'

'Well now, you believe that if you like. But fact is,

there's stray dogs around this town, sniffin' out women day and night, and one is that no-good kid, Dane. He thinks he can have my girl ... but he don't know that I got plans for him, mister Boodle, oh yes!'

'For Christ's sake,' Dane said to himself, 'Get up to bed, Boodle. Throw out the drunk!' But Boodle was drinking as much as the other, and they were clinking glasses and laughing at nothing, finding every remark each one made incredibly amusing. Dane heard noises behind somewhere and had to move quickly to stand behind a door as it opened. It was Perdy, telling them to shut up.

This seemed to get through to Happen Boodle, and he told Elias that it was time for bed. He led him to the bolted door and said goodnight. Any minute now he would be climbing the stairs, and that, thought Joe Dane, would be his walk to heaven or hell.

11

There was another citizen of Broken Man who couldn't sleep that night: Hal Bornless. He was so fixed on his career as an entertainer and humourist that he spent most of his spare time researching the papers and periodicals, looking for markets. He saw himself as a comic artist, and to see his name in print was his ultimate dream. He sat in his pokey little room at the back of the Hoyt place, which he rented for next to nothing, and pored over back issues of the Mid West papers. This night, in the midst of his cursory reading, something caught his eye. It was a familiar face. Looking out at him, with the only difference being a lack of a beard, was the face of Lord Harry Lacey, and the headline above the face read, 'Lawman guns down the Munter Boys.' Hal Bornless read the piece, so astounded that his jaw dropped:

The sheriff of Silver Float, Lord Harry Lacey, the English aristocrat gun-slinger, faced up to the Munter brothers yesterday and shot both men dead. The Munters had run a reign of terror across O'Neill's Valley, instilling fear into local miners and their families, and they showed no respect for the law. Only last month, Carey Munter rode his mare into the Silver Flat stores and crushed a man against a wall. 'I don't regret taking lives when the dead in question are scum, almost as low as the scavenging rats of the back yards,' said Sheriff Lacey. . . .'

Hal checked the date. It was just two years back. He chewed over in his mind the consequences of this news, and wondered who should be told. The man of peace was not what he seemed. Now he definitely couldn't sleep, and he read the piece over again, beginning to believe it now. How many more men had Lacey killed, he asked himself. Here was this fine-living, upright literary speaker, a man apparently beyond the reach of the scandal-mongers, a man with all the cultivated personality of the old-time lords of the manors, and here he was, living a lie! They had to be told, the club members, they had to know about this impostor. He had come out west with his civilized values and his fancy talk, and all the time he was a man of straw, he was no better than a spectacle at a zany show in the travelling feast. He was that hollow. They would have to be told about him.

At the Big Question, Carney now had the attention of Doc Potworthy, who resented being dragged out of bed at such an hour. He had Carney carried from the floor, where he lay when the Doc and Will arrived, to the bed, and there he examined him.

'You've prodded every damned inch of me, Doc, and now you need to do . . . somethin' as I'm, I'm fightin' for breath here, mister!'

'Mr Carney, you have a faulty heart. The outlook is not good. Fortunately I have some of my Golden Medicine with me. . . .'

'Oh, not that again, Doc. You gave me that last time and I was sick for days . . . the room stank with it. Can't you try something else?'

The Doc stroked his chin. 'Mr Carney . . . I'll take some blood. Too much blood surgin' through the guts, that's bad. Your poor heart has too much work to do. Now I have some wonderful little fellers, these leeches, in my bag here. . . .'

'Go ahead . . . Will, bring some whiskey, quick.' Carney accepted his fate. But inside he was planning and scheming. It was going to be a big face-up, a confrontation. No more back-talk and little brawls. It was time to put an end to it all. Soon, after some blood was taken and some of a nasty brown brew was forced down his throat, he went into a half-sleep and he waited till the Doc had gone before calling for Will, who came to sit by him.

'Will, we have to learn from this. I'm not gonna live for ever. I'm gonna be on my feet tomorrow, and then the day after, we're taking the boys into town, all of 'em except the minders for the steers and the old-timers spitting baccy into dust. We're gonna end it.'

'If that's what you want, boss, then yeah.'

'Well, I been thinking of Red . . . I mean how he died. To think of him dying there, stretched on the floorboards of McCoy's rank old jail! To think of it, Will! Now I'm gonna sleep, and I'm getting up in the mornin' to work it out, then the next day, close it all, you wait and see.'

Will just told him to sleep, but he knew his boss from years back, and he knew that this time he meant it. Too long the old man had simmered and stewed that need for revenge, that rancid taste of being wronged, and the urgent desire to get even – it had been seeping through him for far too long. If he had a bad heart, then it was down to that damned sheriff and his cruelty.

In The False Start, Joe Dane was standing behind the open door that led to a corridor. Coming up the main stairs, the worse for drink and singing to himself, was Happen Boodle; he was moving slowly, then stopped altogether and looked around, waiting for the strength to move his legs. In that instant on the stairs, there was absolute silence in the hotel; everyone slept, from the musicians in their lodging to the girls at the far end of the building, and his own dear Perdy in her room. How he wished he could go to her bed. He was thinking of her as he stopped. Then in that silence he could distinctly hear breathing.

Behind the door, Dane was waiting till the footsteps came close, then he would step out and lunge at the older man, pushing him backwards. If the fall didn't kill him, then a pistol-whipping would.

Boodle sensed the presence of someone or something. He whispered, 'Who's that? What kind of rat is skulking there? Show yourself.'

There was no reply, and he made the mistake of moving up to the top step and then stretched a leg towards the door. In seconds the door was swung closed and it slammed Boodle in the face. He staggered, but didn't fall back. Dane came at him and kicked him in the belly. Boodle lost all control of his body and there was no time to grasp anything to cling to. He rolled back and tumbled down the stairs, hitting the bottom rail hard with his head – and then his body lay on its back, his eyes staring up towards the high ceiling.

Luckily for Dane, it had not been a noisy fall. He went down, quick, and checked that the man was dead. There seemed to be no pulse, but he wasn't certain, so slammed a sharp blow with the grip of his pistol on the temple. Then there was no time to lose. He made for the main door,

unbolted it and ran off. There was no sound anywhere, and no sign of anyone moving around. It
was an occasion when he was grateful that the
town lawmen were so useless at their work. A
bunch of comancheros could have ridden into
town, cut throats, robbed coffers and ridden off
without a lawman stirring.

There was a roll of dollars in Joe Dane's pocket,
and room enough for another roll now that it had
been earned. Nothing quite so easy as takin' a life
he thought, as he made for the Big Question and
another satisfied customer. People would find a
poor old drunk who had fallen down the stairs.
Terrible shame, they would say. Yes, life is so fragile.
No, he thought, nothing quite so easy as taking a
life.

When he reached the ranch, Will Ringo was
waiting for him, aiming to make sure that he knew
the score regarding Carney's plans. He took care of
the horse and then took Dane to one side.

'Tomorrow . . . it's a day for working out the way
to win . . . then the next mornin', my boy, we're
rubbin' out McCoy and his boys for good.'

'No, no. I have to take care of McCoy. I been
employed for that. He's my business . . . I resolve
him. The pay's for me.'

'Sure. That will be in the plan, my friend. Clean
your barrels. Steady your hands. You got tomorrow
to think it through.'

Dane had no need. It would be the usual professional job, with no risks. McCoy would be shot in the back. Nobody paid him for heroics. They paid for results.

12

The Literary Club were meeting after breakfast the next day, and they gathered outside The False Start – only to be greeted by Perdy and a group of workers, who led them to the body of Happen Boodle, still lying on the floor, with Doc Potworthy bending over him. As the crowd gathered, and questions were asked, the Doc said, 'Had a fight, I'd say, and either fell or was pushed down the stairs . . . full of booze. I can smell it now.'

Voices muttered, 'No, he was always moderate in his drink' and 'Surely Boodle wouldn't go that way . . . he was a cautious man!' He had been well liked, and everybody, as they heard about his death, wanted to be there, to be near where he was, and to find out the circumstances. Alby Groot, always a stirrer and a lover of trouble, added, 'I never saw Boodle down more than four long drinks at a sitting, he was so moderate a character!'

Preacher Hoyt put an arm around Perdy, and sat

her down. Her sobs filled the room, echoing across the silent dance floor. Her girls stood around, offering help and giving soothing words.

Into this scene came Harry Lacey, and he had been troubled as soon as he woke up that morning. This was his last day in Broken Man before he was due to move on west, but he had been profoundly affected by the shooting of Lydia and by the problems besetting the town. Now, as he dressed and thought about food, he was asking himself some questions about what he could do to help. It was clear to him that the place was caught in a situation he knew well. He had seen it before. At the core of the dissension there was one burning hatred, and everything else was edgy, apprehensive all the time, every minute of the day.

The moaning and weeping before him as he walked into the saloon did not help at all. There was a crowd around a body – he could tell that, because a pair of legs was visible. Only as he went closer could he make out that it was Mr Boodle, and he saw Perdy, still crouched over her man's chest, sobbing and moaning.

A death, and a violent one: he knew then that somehow, beyond rational explanation, he had been expecting this. It was down to something in the atmosphere of the place – bad blood infects. He always thought that.

Doc Potworthy came to him and explained the situation. 'Fell down the stairs . . . probably drunk.

Tragic . . . tragic, my Lord Harry . . . typical of this barbarous wasteland. . . .'

Harry moved closer and ranged his look over the body: something he had done a hundred times. He had lived close to death for so long, and he knew all the signs that the Grim Reaper left, to show his route into the snatch of the body into his own dark realms beyond what men knew. His gaze stopped and fixed on some blood on the floor and on Perdy's hand as she lifted Boodle's head to kiss his face.

He moved around to stand behind Perdy and sure enough, there it was – a wound, showing clearly that the man had been hit very hard by something, and that something left a mark familiar to Harry. He had been bludgeoned by a pistol grip. Chances are he had received the blows when he hit the floor, probably after fighting or being attacked on the stairs. The signs of that included the placing of his arms, which were as they would be when we try to break a fall. But then, he could have struggled with someone first, up at the top. All that mattered though, is what was obvious, Harry thought: he had been bludgeoned by something, most likely a pistol.

'Doc . . .' he said, turning to Potworthy, who was cleaning his glasses and paying no attention to anything. 'Doc . . . this man was murdered.'

'What . . . murdered you say?' The Doc realized that heads had turned and everyone had heard what was being said.

'You didn't look too close, Doc. See the back of the head . . . been whipped by a gun. I'd say a solid sort of pistol . . . maybe army issue . . . makes a good clubbing weapon.'

When Perdy heard this she got to her feet and moved from sorrow to rage. 'Killed? My only good friend, *murdered* did you say, Lord Harry?' She came to him and looked him in the eyes. 'I'm afraid to say, ma'am, that I seen plenty of these wounds. Most killers are cowards, and that's the coward's way . . . I'd say he did fall down the stairs . . . most likely pushed by the killer.'

Perdy shouted and wailed and thumped her fists on the strong chest of the tall aristocrat, her head finally resting on his shirt as she had sobbed until it seemed her heart was worn out and her anger calmed. Harry held her and tried to find some words to console her, but there was nothing that would help.

Perdy then pulled away. Wiping her face clear of tears with the bandana that Harry had offered her, she snapped out, 'If he was killed, then there's a killer, and I want his neck stretched. Do we have law in this town or not?'

Hal and Chet tried to take her close and say comforting things, but she pulled away. Voices started whispering names, all related to Itch Carney. 'He wouldn't do this himself, folks . . . but well, we know how he works. He had no time for Happen!'

Suddenly Perdy called out, as if a stab of truth

had wounded her. ' 'Course . . . I've just turned the man down! I told him . . . I mean, I told him that Happen was . . . was a better man, that I might marry Happen . . . and now!'

'Don't jump to wild conclusions, Perdy,' Harry said.

'They're wild conclusions because they're about a wild man!' she said, wiping away tears.

Finally, after a long gap of time, McCoy arrived, having been told about what had happened. He was about to offer a weak apology when Perdy yelled at him, 'Where were you when this happened? You're not a lawman . . . you're not even a real man, McCoy. Do they pay you in pieces of silver?'

McCoy did the only thing he could do: he ignored her and moved across to look at the body. The Doc now took his new information and made more of it. 'Sheriff, this is the work of the bastard who pesters this town like fleas around a carcass . . . Itch Carney. It's a plain case of murder, Sheriff . . . see the wound there?'

McCoy bent and took a close look, then nodded and groaned something about making an arrest but having no proof. He asked the crowd in general, 'Anybody see this?'

At first there were no answers, but then Chet Two Winds said, 'I could say that I saw it, boss!' A chorus of other voices said the same thing.

The mumbles continued, with Carney's name being repeated and maligned. Harry, who had been deep in thought and feeling the tugs of conscience about doing something in the town, which was obviously languishing under a dark star, now needed some time to think, and he needed a drink or two as he did so. Chet Two Winds saw his expression and asked what he could do. Soon they were at the bar along the street, the beer-shop with a few benches and sawdust on the floor. A fat old man put large whiskies in front of them and resisted an urge to smile.

Chet spoke first, after the whiskies were downed. 'I'm supposed to be at the literary club meeting any time now, Harry. But I wanted to be sure you're all right. I mean, you're leaving us in the morning, I believe?'

'We'll see. Just leave me to think now, eh?' Leaving the place didn't seem right, he was thinking. He had never run from trouble.

Chet Two Winds left him to his thoughts.

At the other end of town, as the sun was now up and beating on every little corner of Broken Man, Lydia had decided to pay her monthly visit to her father's grave in the little fenced cemetery by the one-room cabin that was the makeshift church for the town. In fact, locals called it the worship place, as the term church was too grand a title for it. But the Hoyts had grand plans and were trying to raise funds for the building of something that was unmistakably a church or at least a chapel.

Lydia was bending by her father's wooden cross which had his name written on in white paint: just 'Here lies Rico Santo.' She had been coming to the spot ever since he died, sitting there every month and talking to him, as she was doing today. She put just one little envelope in the dust. It was a letter written to his spirit, and Lydia believed in spirits; she believed that one day she would meet him again and they would talk and hug. Now she said the things that had been running through her mind during the night: 'Pa, I hope your soul is now in Paradise, where it should be, and that you see what's going on down here in this vale of tears . . . for that is what it is now. Pa, sadness fills this place like a slow flood. But there is one good thing to tell you . . . Liza di Buco has found her Bonneville! Oh yes, he's tall, fair and gentle. He's a lord from over the great ocean, and I think he's the one I have dreamed of. . . .'

What she didn't know was that she had a listener nearby. Only a few yards away, crouched by a row of sand-filled bushes, was Joe Dane, and he was not happy about what he heard.

'Lydie, it's me, Joe,' he whispered, and she jumped with fear.

'Joe Dane, you almost made my heart stop! What you doin', sneaking around behind me?'

'I was looking for you, and then I saw you walk in here . . . look, Lydie, we was once real special. You know how we felt about each other.' He sat down next to where she was crouched, speaking to her father's spirit. 'I told you how you was the only girl I would ever need in my life, and you know I speak the truth when I say that since I left Broken Man, there has been no other girl that has had my affections. You have to believe that, darlin'. Some men can lie as natural as they breathe, but . . .'

'Ma says you're one such a man, Joe,' Lydia said, with venom.

He took a little strand of red hyssop that was growing close to the ground, and he handed it to her. 'See, this is for you. It's a beautiful red flower that grows even in this bone-dry scrub – something like you, I'd say!'

Lydia was no fool and she saw the performance in this. At first she played along, but then took the flower and threw it back at him, with an accusation, 'Joe Dane, you left without a word. You just up and left, and all your fine words were worth nothin' . . . not a handful of dry dust.'

He moved away slightly, and Lydia took the chance to ask something she had been longing to ask since Dane came back. 'Now Joe, if you want to do something real fine for me, well, you can tell me something and speak true, as you say you do.'

'Sure, anything . . . just ask.'

'The truth is, I been thinking about how Pa died, ever since you left. I was told about the accident and . . .'

'Right, if you really want to know, but maybe you

should put all that behind you. Live for now, Lydie, like we said we always would.'

Lydia had a feeling that Joe Dane knew much more than he ever said. Something in her wanted to push him, goad him, into emptying out all that he knew, spilling it out and settling matters for good. 'Joe, I know he died on the cattle drive to Cheyenne, but there's been talk. I've heard men talk about that day, and fact is, it don't add up.'

Joe stood up and walked around, kicking dust. Then he seemed to think of the right words to say and he squat down again. 'Lydie, just leave it alone. I was there that day. I saw him fall. That's what it amounts to ... We either have luck, or we don't. There ain't no God. If there is, he don't give a dead rat for us down here in this back-end of nowhere.'

'Joe Dane, you denied the Lord ... and in a graveyard, too!' Lydia was disgusted.

'Lydie ... just think how Broken Man got its name! I mean, the story I was told concerned Carney's grandpa, who came here from down South and things was so bad his family starved, all but one ... Carney's daddy! Now I heard that old grandpa Carney was the man who gave this place its name and put the first post up, telling any arrivals that he had been broke by the darned place.'

'That's a fine old yarn, son, but it stretches the truth, just like you.' Lydia and Joe turned towards the voice, and there stood Elias Hole. His giant frame cast a long, solid shadow, and his face showed that he wasn't too happy. Joe Dane, along with every soul in Broken Man and beyond, knew about Elias Hole's moods and tempers. Along the road of his life there were a number of casualties of his temper; some were still limping to that day, and some were still getting aches in the jaw and pains in the back.

'Now, Mister Dane. I have one very plain thing to say to you, boy. Get out of my sight, out of this town . . . start riding, and don't come back!'

From somewhere deep down, Joe Dane found words of defiance. 'I don't take no heed of threats and commands, Mister Hole.'

'Oh really? How about this? Do you obey this?' He rolled back the sleeve on his right arm and held up a fist, tight and hard and ready to go.

For Joe Dane, this kind of situation was one that prompted the right hand to dart down to the pistol in the holster and whip up the barrel in a split-second, followed by a shot to the heart of any man who faced him and insulted him. But this time, thinking of Lydia present, his hand stopped, hovering over the grip of the gun. In that moment, big Elias kicked out a leg and knocked Dane backwards, where he sprawled over the grave of Rico Santo.

Lydia let out a scream and ran for cover behind the nearest greenery, while Dane ran at Elias, to try a desperate head butt in the belly. But as he discovered, the effect was like a wooden pole ramming up to a thick stone wall: no impact at all, and his unfortunate body merely shivered and then folded. Dane was soon on the earth at the feet of Elias, who picked him up and threw him several feet down the gentle slope of the graveyard. But he gave Dane no time to recover, and when the man struggled to his feet, Elias hit him with a forearm across the nose and then a knee to the guts.

Then there was a real beating dished out, as Elias slugged and battered Dane, throwing him around like a dog with a dead rat. Elias was the kind of man who went hell for leather once he was stirred to action, and not much could restrain him.

'Don't, Pa! Stop! Stop at once!' This was Lydia, and she had now run out to hold on to Elias's thick belt, and tug at it, to get his attention. He gave Dane one last swipe with his fist and the gunman lay out cold like a dead man.

13

Harry was staying in The False Start for his last night in Broken Man. He had wanted to be away from the literary crowd and needed some time to think. He was next booked for the same talk at Daunt's Pass, a day's ride on the stage again, but there was something bothering him: the shot that had injured the young woman, Lydia. What kind of a town was this? Now there was the death of Boodle, and in fact, when it came to supper time, Perdy, who had been sedated and had been sleeping for hours, emerged and walked into the main bar where Harry was sitting alone, watching the card players and trying to understand what was splitting the town apart.

Perdy tapped him on the shoulder, pulled out a chair, and asked, 'Can a poor common singer sit down with an English lord?'

He smiled and welcomed her. 'Sure. Forget the lordship thing. I want to help you if I can. I know what it's like to lose someone close.'

'I'm sure you do,' said Perdy, waving her arm to call for a drink, which soon arrived. 'This is gin, Harry, the only thing that helps when a girl doesn't believe in anything.'

'Have you always felt that way?'

'No, sir . . . I was brought up a good Christian, and I prayed before every meal and went to church twice a week. My pappy was a God-fearing man and a complete fool. He trusted too much, and that's weak. Mind, I have to say I trusted Happen. He was the finest man I ever knew. Should have married him. But I never wanted no man to shove me around and rap out orders . . . you follow?'

'Oh, I follow! In England, everybody except the men who own the land gets told what to do, when to do it, and trust is floating around, an option only for fools.'

Perdy gave Harry a searching look and finished her gin. 'I can't figure you out, stranger. Why do you do these lectures? Do you feel a better man for spouting on about law and justice?'

It was clear that she had hit a nerve. Harry called for a drink now, and as the beer arrived, he explained, 'Miss Perdy, not so long ago I was the kind of man who gave orders, pushed people around, kicked fools out of my way . . . I had learned to survive in a strange land, and I trusted nobody because that was too risky. I'm a one-man enterprise, Miss, and cash for food and clothes is all that counts. Talking about law and justice pays pretty well. Your townsfolk, like so many others like 'em out here, they want a touch of the finer things in life . . . though civilization comes at a cost. A few hundred bucks a visit, in fact.'

'It all sounds very smug. The only thing Happen was smug about was Vienna. He was a man of your culture as well. He could talk day and night about dinners and princes, parades and bands . . . oh, and the poets of the city. He said he was brought up with silver spoons and fancy words. . . .' Perdy's voice began to waver and fade, and a sob rose in her, prompting Harry to put an arm around her and give some comforting words. In the throes of the weeping that rose to fill her cheeks with tears she muttered Happen's name and put her head down on the table.

'Miss Perdy, why don't you go and lie down . . . you're not ready for this.' Harry said.

She pulled herself up sharp, called for more drink, and told Harry not to worry at her like an old dame. Harry, instead of arguing, pulled her to him again and kissed her forehead, saying, 'You know what . . . it would be a fine idea for you to sing us a song . . . maybe Happen's favourite?'

She loved the idea, and she was soon on her feet, shouting for the fiddler who was now dozing in a corner, to come up on to the dance floor and play *I Know Where I'm Going*. Perdy, making the heads turn at the card tables and in the line of serious drinkers at the long bar, spoke first. 'Ladies and gentlemen, this is an old, old song and Happen Boodle loved it.

He used to hum it all the time. . . .' She sang the first lines after the fiddler had played a few bars of the melody: '*I know where I'm going and I know who's going with me . . . I know who I love, but the dear knows who . . . who, I'll marry. . . .*'

Her voice faltered over the last few words, but she picked up again when the audience clapped her, and she sang the song through, until she managed to end with a smile on the same words again: '*But the dear knows who I'll marry. . . .*'

When she sat down by Harry again, she said, 'You know, Lord Harry Lacey, you could stick around. I could use someone to sweep up the straw!' She managed to laugh at this, and Harry joined her. 'Seriously though, mister Lord . . . you must be in need of a little female company sometimes . . . one of my girls could oblige . . . that's all you men want, right?'

She was now struggling to maintain control of her anger, and the sourness was coming through the usually polite, professional exterior behaviour.

'Some of us don't think like that, Miss Perdy.'

'Oh, some of us don't, do we? Some of us is too grand for a little missy from Colorado, eh?'

The fiddler saved the moment from more trouble and embarrassment by asking the band to join him in some of Happen's favourite dance tunes. Soon Perdy and Harry were stepping around the floor, to the applause of the drunks, drifters and cowboys.

*

When Itch Carney finally made it out of bed and faced what was to him a hostile world, he reminded himself that in twenty-four hours destiny would arrive, at least for the Son of Satan who existed in the jailhouse. Itch thought, with a thrill of satisfaction, how the sun rising on the next morning would be the last dawn that McCoy would ever see.

He needed to take the day to gather strength, to muster his resources – fine, so he couldn't suddenly be the fighter he was when he first came out west twenty years back, but he could still pull a trigger and fire straight and true. He thought of how close he had been to death just a year before, when he had had that collapse. It had been a warning to him, he thought now, a warning to act, instead of letting time roll on and the hunger to make McCoy pay go on gnawing at him.

It was the full light of late morning around him when he pulled his clothes on over his aching bones, and stood by the long old mirror that had been his Ma's. He didn't like what he saw. Who was that weak old man? It was in the face and in the frame that he saw the age. But no, he had to take heart, for this one last throw of the dice.

He shouted for Will, who was over the way in the stables, and as he called out, he staggered forward and felt a pain in his chest. He supported his weight on the table, pressing on it hard, so the thick wood

101

would take the force. Then, slowly, he recovered, just in time to put a smile on his face as Will Ringo came to the door. 'You wanted me, boss?'

'Yeah, Will. Come on in and sit there. Now, I want to run through tomorrow's preparations.'

'Mr Carney, we have eighteen hands ready and willin'. How can we fail?'

' 'Course we can fail, son. Every general on campaign knew the concern for possible defeat. You never read about Napoleon? Now there's a man who covered all possible flaws in strategy – see what he achieved!'

Will wanted to remind Carney that this was not some great battlefield, but just a baking hot, dead corner of Colorado, which folk with any sense would see and then ride on past, but he could understand that his boss's feelings for the sheriff had rankled in him like a new burn, and he settled for a nod and a smile.

'Will, who's the bastard got with him?'

'I'm pretty sure there's four deputies, and of course there's Elias Hole, and he's worth three men in a fight.'

'That all? Six men against our twenty-one?'

'Not quite that simple, Boss. You see, lessen we act real sharp, the Broken Man Godly types and dark suits, they're gonna cluster around their tin star. There's Chet Two Winds and there's Hal Bornless . . . even some of the regulars at The False Start, since Boodle died and faces turn your way in suspicion.'

He stopped talking as Itch Carney cut in with, 'Oh yeah . . . thanks for reminding me that Happen Boodle is no more. The boys told me about it. Terrible shame! 'Course it was a sad accident and can't be blamed on me. So none of the saloon and hotel crowd is gonna point the finger this way?'

'No boss, it was a pure accident and nothing to do with Joe Dane . . . shame for Miss Perdy!' He said this with a wry smile and a strong sense of sarcasm.

'Exactly. Miss Perdy, she's surely looking for some consolation in the arms of, well, maybe some old son of sin who runs a ranch, name of Carney!' He laughed so loud as he said this that his yellow teeth showed in the light, and Will Ringo joined in.

'So, as I was saying Will, I make the arithmetic notably in our favour. Tell the boys to be ready, with rifles and pistols checked and smooth, after first eats tomorrow. We go straight for the jail and shoot it into pieces. Splinters will fly! A volley from some Winchesters should split some wood. By full sun we'll have bodies feeding flies and rats. Any prisoners in that place, Will, it's too bad for them.'

'Coffee boss?'

Carney still felt flashes of pain across his chest and was pushing himself to cover over the evidence of that deep hurting that was likely to show on his weather-beaten face. The coffee helped. And so did the drug that Doc Potworthy had left for him – the usual laudanum. He took the coffee, thick and strong as mud, and told Will that he needed rest again, before they met up to eat, when Joe Dane would be due to show up.

'I'm going to town tonight, Boss. Just a game of cards, but I'm listening for every scrap of talk I can hear.'

'Right, but nice and easy, you savvy? Keep real quiet about everything. We want a normal feel to life. No sign of a storm brewing, eh?'

'Sure. What's more normal than Will Ringo playing some poker?'

14

In The False Start, Perdy and Harry were still together, and Harry was trying his best to help her through the worst time of her life – coping with the loss of her man. By early evening she had slowed down the rate of taking in wine or gin, but she was the worse for wear, and moody. The staff did their best, as they knew all her moods, and one by one they tried to get her to rest. As for Harry, he relied on talk, and in the past he had found that to be the best medicine.

He managed somehow to bring in two of the girls who worked there, and the fiddler, and he tried to turn the conversation to something that would keep Perdy away from the extremes of her mood, but it was no use. She suddenly threw her glass across the room and said, 'So who's the coward who killed my Boodle then? Who killed my little German?'

One of the girls answered, 'Easy . . . Itch Carney, though he didn't do it himself.'

'She's right. It was that no good shameless failure . . . I turned him down, you know that everybody? I turned him down, and he went off like a little red-faced boy being told he can't have no cherry pie!'

Harry sensed that feeling of helplessness he had known so many times. But then Perdy stood up and walked around to Harry, sat down on his lap and started to run a finger along his cheek, down under his chin.

'Harry Lacey, you're the kind of man I should be with. I mean you got some style, some manners . . . men around here, they treat you like you're a crate of goods to shunt around. But you, well you're a true man of courage and honour. You know why folks? Because he has no gun attached to that strong leather belt there . . . he's not a man of violence. Now ain't that courage?'

'Some might say it was foolish!' someone said. Harry took up the point. 'True mister, some would be right to say that. I can see that the gun is the law out here. Yet things can be different. There are other ways to run things. . . .'

Perdy stood up now and rapped out, 'Tell that to Happen Boodle . . . you know what, mister English Lord? He won't hear ya!'

The musicians and the girls agreed that this would be a good time for them to play and dance again, to lighten the mood and distract Perdy from her misery. It was around the time when things livened up a little at The False Start, but with there being a shadow of death over the place, maybe things would be different, the girls thought. They were wrong. Soon, just after the band played again, in came Will Ringo and a bunch of cow hands from the Big Question. Will did all the right things: he went to Perdy and expressed his condolences, very formal and proper. The other boys did the same. They could see that now she was much the worse for drink, sitting and trying concentrate on the band, with Harry next to her, ready to help.

Will eyed him, and his brain was busy with possible situations about the tall stranger. He decided to play a bold hand. 'Mister Lacey . . . you here tomorrow?'

'No. I'm catching the first stage west. Another job waiting. . . .'

'Fine. I wish you good luck.' He held out a hand and Harry shook it. Will was relieved that there was one less potential ally for McCoy and the officials of the town.

'We're gonna play some poker, Miss Perdy,' Will said, 'But I appreciate that you're mourning a fine man, and we'll be real orderly, that's a promise.'

At that moment, in came McCoy and he heard the last words. 'Oh, really? A Carney cowpoke promising good behaviour? Life has its surprises.'

'I don't want no trouble, Sheriff. Me and the boys . . . we're playing cards and sipping cool beer. That's all it amounts to.'

'I expect respect for Mr Boodle and his good

partner here, Miss Perdy. I know it's a saloon bar, but some manners and quiet would be fine.'

'Rest easy, McCoy. You just enjoy a placid sort of evening. You never know when you'll have another.'

The Big Question boys knew the innuendo of that, and they couldn't resist smiles, but nothing else was said.

Harry could never understand the appeal of gambling. As he sat with Perdy, Chet Two Winds arrived and it was clear that he was of the same mind. Chet came to offer help and support, and Harry soon came to see that there was more to the literary club than met the eye. Chet may have been one for tall tales, but he had seen life and he knew people. When he arrived, he saw straightaway that Perdy wasn't really happy with the noise from the card players, who by that time had taken too much to drink along with the passions of the play – even Will, usually the foreman, was sounding off about something, and there was the kind of row you get from men who have been bored too long and need some kind of release.

Chet said, 'I came to see if there's anything I can do, Miss Candle, seeing as I'm verging on being the old timer around here, and as I was a friend to Mr Boodle, and him to me. Why we rode together once, all the way from La Junta, after he went to sell some valuables . . . he was raising cash to buy this place.'

There was a shout from the card table, and then

some bad language. Chet stood up and strode across to the boys from the Big Question. He stood firm and spoke direct, 'Now boys, you must see that openin' the place today was a special concession to the town. Miss Perdita Candle by rights should be just mournin' and be shut away to cope with her sorrow. So this kind of rowdy behaviour will just not do.'

'Oh really? It won't do? So suddenly you're the man who runs the place, are you? Or maybe you're the new sheriff, as the present one is a snivellin' coward and a man who neglects his charges so that they die on him. Which are you, you pain in the backside?' This was Will Ringo, and he had forgotten that he promised Carney he would behave and just watch things, so he could report back.

'I think you're rude and you need teachin' some manners, Ringo.' Chet showed no fear. But unfortunately the Carney boys had no regard for that, and the three men with Will got to their feet and started grabbing Chet. He hit one of them and then staggered back as another ran for his midriff. When Chet clattered against the wall and squealed in pain, it was time for Harry to act.

The gamblers were holding Chet still while Will Ringo was reaching to crack a fist across his face. 'You no-good half-breed, with your fancy high-minded shams, you're gonna pay for your damned cheek!'

But in a second, Harry took hold of Ringo's arm

and spun him round, then punched him hard in the face. He went down with a cry of pain. Harry ripped one of the men off Chet, who now struggled with odds of two to one. In the midst of all this Perdy shouted for Sheriff McCoy.

Harry saw that the man taking him on was about to reach for a knife, and as soon as he grasped the handle, Harry gave a strong kick at the blade and dislodged it so it spun across the floor. By now Perdy was yelling for them to stop, but Chet was losing against two men, and Harry had his man fast and secure, with an arm behind his back and giving threats of breaking the arm if he didn't stop fighting.

Just as Will Ringo recovered and got to his feet, and swung a fist at Harry's cheek, the voice of McCoy rang out across the room, 'Stop this at once!'

The Big Question boys ran for the back door, throwing Chet to one side. But Harry grabbed Will Ringo, and McCoy took over, telling the two deputies who were following him to take Ringo into custody.

'You been irritatin' me for too long, Ringo. I've let too many things pass. But this time I'm lockin' you up. Being first man to that son of Satan out there don't give you immunity from the law. Take him away, boys.'

'Not for long, McCoy. Your life is near its limit. Better fear the hours ticking away!' Ringo spat out the words and gave McCoy a look of sheer contempt.

He was hauled away, and McCoy turned to Harry and Perdy, 'Now you two, how about you close up and take some time away from the place, eh? You all right, son?' He was looking at Harry, whose face was dribbling blood. 'I can see your right eye is gonna swell something bad.'

Perdy said she would take care of him, and the sheriff left. But Harry was turning over in his mind what Ringo had said. It didn't sound like a general statement: it was more like a threat, as if he knew there was a problem coming along, due soon like a loco expected along the line.

But Harry had no more time to think. Perdy called for some ointment and for her 'emergency box' as she always called it. One of the girls brought it, and in her other hand she had a small rock: 'See, Miss Perdy, look what was in that drawer . . . the mad-stone!'

'Of course, Lord Harry, I have to tell you that this rock was one of Happen's most crazy little habits, and he was some eccentric I have to say! 'Twas the nearest thing to a weapon the man had . . . he was after your own heart, a man of peace. But he was known to have slammed it on to someone's head, when roused.' She managed a laugh, and Harry could see that she was bringing to mind a fine memory of Boodle.

'I'm putting on my special ointment . . . that's a

111

hell of a bruise, Lord Harry . . . but I know all about looking after men. Years of practice have made me an expert at nursing. So sit down here, good . . . now lie back. This is called a chaise longue and it always added some class to the place.'

He did lie back, and she gently treated the bruise, and mopped up the blood. 'Faces always bleed some, that's for sure. But it looks worse than it is . . .'

His thoughts went to the next day, and what he was to do. Dusk had crept into the Colorado evening; there was barely any sound out in the street. His mind ranged over what he had seen since coming here: the girl being shot, and then a man killed in his own home. Now another brawl. Was it right to move on, to leave the town to its destiny? Harry Lacey had always believed that a man makes his own luck. Was the coming day the right time to test out that theory? But for the time being, the soft hands of a beautiful woman were gliding along his jaw, and then dabbing something that stung on a cut below one eye. Her perfume filled his nose, and then his whole sense of being.

By the end of the night, as a coyote bayed at the moon, and he and Perdy had been left alone, sitting in a corner seat, still sipping beer in his case, and in hers, more red wine drunk, to suppress the thoughts of the man she had lost.

'You asleep, Miss Perdy?' Harry asked, softly.

'Very nearly. I think my mind is spinning . . . but

112

you know, I have a welcoming bed upstairs. I could use some comfort.'

He accepted, but as they went into bed, and the woman nestled close to him, he sensed that she was slipping into a restful sleep. He just held her. *Harry Lacey,* he whispered, to no one but himself, *how long since you had the warmth of a woman by you? Too long, Mister Drifter, too long . . . but goodnight lady.*

15

The literary club had barely started their conversation, and Chet Two Winds, in spite of cuts and bruises on his face and a sore head, was in full flow recounting his days in the mines when the Chiracahua Apaches arrived looking for blood, with Alby Groot calling him a liar, when Hal Bornless rushed in, panting with his news.

'Hey listen! I have something to tell you all. Lord Harry Lacey . . . he's a killer!'

Heads turned and there were gasps. Mrs Hoyt was visibly shocked, and her husband had to stop her going into one of her fainting episodes.

'The man of culture, the one who stood and talked about the need for peace and true justice, that man has taken lives! I thought you all should know.'

'Well, we ain't paid him yet. He's due to come here any time now and take his dollars away with him to his next lecture date.' This was Preacher

Hoyt, and he spoke the words with a sense of grievance. It was the troublemaker, Alby Groot, who seized the chance to stir it up: 'Right, I'm not going to be a member of a society that issues a contract with a known desperado. I knew as soon as he walked in that he was a refined and died-in-the-wool liar. Didn't I tell you that, Mrs Hoyt?'

She had no time to reply.

'Just one blamed, dashed minute!' said Doc Potworthy, 'Mr Bornless, you need to substantiate this wild claim . . . we all know you're a romancer and like to spin a three-volume novel out of a dime yarn!'

'Substantiate! Why, it's here in print. I combed the press for this scandal and you know what? He had blood on his hands . . . the blood of seven men, now under the sods, and him a self-proclaimed man of peace!'

'Maybe we withhold the payment?' Mrs Hoyt said.

'No way can we do that. Word will get around that Broken Man folk are two-faced crooks! Anyway, I like the man. He saved me from a beating yesterday . . . I mean, a worse beating, or worse. . . .' Chet said this with his usual tone of passionate dissent.

The Doc raised an arm for quiet and Preacher Hoyt called for hush. Then Mrs Hoyt, recovered from the shock now, said, 'Now listen, fellow authors and people of culture and learning, we have had an impostor amongst us, a charlatan, but he's moving on today, and we're well rid of him.

Consequently we pay up and say nothing.'

'But Lord Harry Lacey is lying to us ... he's a rogue. Probably not even a Lord anyways,' shouted Hal, and waited for a response. But at that second, Lord Harry walked into the room.

Preacher Hoyt took it upon himself to explain. 'Lord Harry, Mr Bornless here is claiming that you are a murderer. Would you care to defend your reputation?'

'No sir, I would not. My life is my own business. Bornless, do tell us more.'

Hal went to stand before the group, and Harry stood with one long leg resting on a chair, listening, but knowing exactly what was coming.

'Lord Harry Lacey, as you see him standing there, shows no sign that he has been a man of violence. You'll note that he carries no gun. The belt around his waist has no sheath and knife. This is the man who spoke to us lately of what justice was, and how firearms bring nothing but death and suffering. Well, the periodicals do not lie, and I have here, copied from a number of such, proof that he was a gunfighter, and he did time in jail. Isn't it typical of this wild place, way distant from the reach of true values, that a no-good bounty hunter should blow in like a weed?'

'Stop!' Harry shouted at him. 'Enough ... I'll explain, now that I have to.' The listeners turned to look at Harry now, and he had their full attention.

'Every man changes his values through his life,

116

and I changed mine. When I first crossed the ocean and put my feet down on this new world, I had to find ways to survive, to feed myself, and the time came when a bullet or a blade was necessary or I would have perished. I never enjoyed it. The fact is, I stooped pretty low and I took lives. But I paid for that and I became a different man. The man in those stories, Mr Bornless, is a stranger to me.'

'So you're asking for forgiveness, Lacey?' Preacher Hoyt asked.

'No. Only God can do that. All I want from you people is some understanding. Now, I'm going to leave my fee with you. Give it to the needy. I'll be across the way, stepping on to the stage west by the late morning. Until then, I'm resting and writing my journal of travels taken. It's the pen, not the gun, today.'

He stopped talking and left the room, leaving behind him an uneasy silence. This lasted for a while, and then the literary types all rattled off their moral opinions, none of them, as usual, agreeing with any of the others. But Chet Two Winds did say again:

'That man probably saved my life yesterday. That's all I can say, folks. Anyway, since when did Hal Bornless do anything upright and moral? He's a darn scribe, a tale-teller down to his marrow. You believe what he says, after the Oxbow Valley fiasco? You'll recall that he came home from that and reported that a thousand Apaches had taken over

117

the valley and murdered every man and woman in sight? Turned out to be three men died in a drunken brawl.'

Nothing else was said. Even Bornless was stuck for words.

The night before, at the Hole house, Lydia and her family were still worried about the bullet wound in the girl's arm, and about the recent trouble from Joe Dane. Ma Lil was tucking up the patient in bed, but sleep was not going to come so willingly. Lydia was troubled, and she asked, 'Ma, I need to ask about my real Pa, about Rico.'

'Yes, my love?'

'I'd like you to tell me how he died.'

'I've told you. Your new Pa told you as well, girl.'

'Yes, but I don't think I have the whole story.'

Ma Lil stroked Lydia's forehead, and then ran a hand through the girl's long hair and told her how beautiful she was, and how men would long for her, better men than Joe Dane.

'You're not answering! You're not listening!' Lydia pushed Ma Lil's hand away and sat up. 'I'm not a child. I need the truth.'

Ma Lil sighed and sat down to face Lydia, looking her straight in the eyes. 'Now, Lydie, your father was caught in a stampede. He was trying to cut out some steers during the worst of it and his horse's hoof caught in something. He was crushed by the beasts. . . . You were told that, and it's true.'

Lydia decided to come out with her worry, and put the question boldly, 'So Joe Dane had nothing to do with it?'

She could see from Lil's face that this was near the mark; it had some truth in it. But then her expression changed and Ma Lil said, 'He was *there*, with Rico, that's all. He was, they said, lucky to escape the same fate. There was some talk . . . some talk about Joe falling out with your Pa over some kind of gambling debt. Just talk. You get that on the trail.'

Lydia was left to sleep, but her thoughts turned to that fatal drive and the stampede. Time passed, and restlessly she turned and turned in her bed, finally getting up and going for some water. It was then that she heard the voices: it was Ma Lil and Elias talking, and she caught the word 'Dane'.

She was flat against the wall, in shadow, so no glow of light from the oil lamp could catch a flicker of her movement. Now she could make out every word.

'She'll go on asking, Lil. She knows there's Joe Dane in the picture somewhere.'

'Sure Elias, you know and I know, that he pushed Rico off the chestnut. He had every reason, mainly that hundred bucks he owed Rico. You can't pay cash to a dead man.'

Elias answered with a sigh, 'I knew when that stray dog showed up again here that there would be trouble. . . . Just when the girl was leavin' all the pain behind, that little rebel turns up.'

'Yes, but at least she sees him for what he is now – no good, a waster and a man fated to dance on the end of a rope!'

'Right, Lil. You couldn't prove it in a court of law, but I'd bet my last nickel that Dane shoved Rico to his death.'

'She'll keep on asking, Elias, she's worse nor a prairie dog for digging out, and she'll drag out the truth like a stored carcass.'

Lydia had heard enough. All her suspicions had been proved. They had been keeping the truth from her. Now, it was time to do something about it. Back she went to bed, her heart thumping and a wave of passionate hate running through her. What she had been suspecting was the case. Why didn't they tell her the facts? Why was the entire world poisoned by the bad blood of lies and deception? It could only be that they feared she might do something extreme. Well, they were right in that, she thought. Something extreme was going to happen, and nothing would stop her doing it. She had always thought that love and hate were two sides of the same coin. The love shone and dazzled you, but the hate was always in the dark side, like there was shame involved. Not this time, though. No shame in wanting Joe Dane dead.

Harry Lacey would help. He was her Bonneville after all. He was a gentleman of the kind you never saw around Broken Man. No, he was like a medieval knight. Back in the time of chivalry, like it said in the school-books, he would have been jousting, with her standard over him and her favour tucked in his armour. Yes, she would find her Bonneville and together they would find vengeance.

In the jailhouse, the day began with coffee and with Will Ringo ranting and shouting to be sent home. McCoy and Elias enjoyed the coffee, and they both grinned at the sight of the Big Question man in such a state of panic.

'Hey, this ain't like you, Ringo, acting like a stuck hog and whinin' like some mother-seeking calf.' This was Elias, who had nothing but contempt for the man. McCoy, though, was interested in the undercurrent of Ringo's threats. 'If you don't let me out and send me home, McCoy, well, let's just say that the law might change sides, if you get my drift.'

'Change sides?'

'Well, maybe it's better to say it could cut the cards in favour of the smartest player. Life is like that poker game, McCoy, and you're a less than average player, we all know that.'

'You're guilty of assault, Ringo. Shut up and take it like a man!' Elias snapped, throwing his coffee dregs towards the jail bars.

'Oh, you're the big man, aren't you, Hole? That's when you're in that position, with me locked in here. But that ain't always the case, and I'd back myself agin you in a face-off, mister, any time.'

'He always did fancy himself as a gunslinger, didn't he, Mister McCoy?' Elias asked, then said that in a fist-fight, Ringo would beg for mercy. 'You ain't no real man, Ringo . . . you're Carney's little dog, the brute he kicks around. . . .'

'Enough you two . . . enough!' McCoy said, finishing his coffee and going to the door. 'I have some business with Preacher Hoyt. He's sent some message about the English Lord. Creggan's coming to keep you company, Elias.'

As he walked out, Deputy Creggan came inside and winked at the prisoner. Creggan was a wind-lashed old cow-hand who had done the big drives north more times than he cared to recall, and he'd been a miner and a stage driver. Now he was wearing the tin star and his skill with a gun was highly valued by McCoy. On that fateful morning, neither of them had any idea just how tested that skill would be.

16

At the Big Question, Itch Carney was cursing. 'Damn it all, son, I told him to keep quiet, to listen and watch, to come back with no trouble hanging over him! It was such a simple instruction. But he had to go and trample down a sound plan. Never would have made a soldier, that boy. Now he's in McCoy's jail . . . where Red died.' He was talking to a bunch of his hands, who were now close to mounting and riding out with him, to settle things with McCoy. They were waiting for Carney to join them, but he had stalled, because he was in pain again, and he didn't want that to show. It was essential that the men saw him well and strong.

He took more coffee and a little laudanum. Since he had stirred that morning, all he could think of was his brother Red's face in the coffin, and the rotten, scarred face of that animal, McCoy. Oh, this was the day of reckoning, and nothing could go wrong. It was with a supreme effort of willpower that he went out, showing the bravado of a much younger man. He grabbed hold of his rifle and aimed a bullet into the air. The horses stirred a little. The men shouted at him. Then he swung a leg up over the saddle on his pinto, his best and speediest mount, and screamed out, 'Come on boys . . . let's pay him back for my kid brother, yeah?'

There was a chorus of 'yeah' from along the line, and the massive force of men lined up in front of their boss.

Joe Dane had never before felt so much like a wounded animal hiding in its lair. In time gone by he had been compared to a predator – a hunter. A resolution man was a human hunter of course, and he had learned to know the scent of fear when he was in pursuit of a quarry.

Now, though, he was licking his wounds, and his beating at the hands of Elias Hole was smarting inside, even more than the stabs of pain he felt from the bruises. If the man hadn't been Lydia's new father, he would have ended him, as he had done her first and real pa. It had taken some effort of will not to pull a revolver on the man and bring him down. So here he was, squatting in some backyard on the outskirts of town, with wounds on arms, back and chest, but with a desire in his heart to get even with that giant block of muscle who was considerably overdue for a slice of humiliation, such as the ones he usually dished out.

It was now the deepest cloak of night around him, and even more, he had a frame of mind close to a coyote bleeding from a fight with a rival, than to a man. All he could think of was that thick-skulled chancer who had shamed him. Maybe the girl was doomed to be an orphan for a second time. He could do nothing but lie still and wait for the first sign of sun-up. Carney would be expecting him, to share the food and then take his place with the cattleman's private army. What he kept telling himself was that, though Carney had any number of men who were useful with a gun, he had chosen Joe Dane to do the job. This was no ordinary assignment, as McCoy was always surrounded by deputies. He rarely strode out alone, and if he did, it was in the dusk or in the thick of night.

But the attack tomorrow would be head on. It would be a siege, and it would be won by volleys of rifle fire and sheer force of numbers, and with no set targets – except for McCoy, who would have to be *his* man.

Though he was hurting bad, Joe Dane knew that this was his best chance of making something of himself. The money would be enough to take him and Lydie away somewhere, for a new beginning. He could wash up some place where he was not known as a wanted man.

The morning would bring his new life, he just knew. But first he would lie, look at the moon, and try to sleep. The folks out there had not the slightest inkling of what was going to hit them the next day. Yes, he thought, it was time for Joe Dane to make things happen.

By around eight, Will Ringo could stand the pretence no longer. Keeping quiet and going along with routine was impossible. He just had to tell McCoy and his men what was coming their way. Since a plate of cold beans and dry bread early in the day, he had held in all that tormenting detail about Carney's plans for the jail. It was when he saw the three of them together around the big table – Creggan, Elias and the young one, Sims – that he let fly something to disturb the peace.

' 'Course, you know that come about noon, this place is certain to be flattened to the ground, and you men with it.'

'Why's that, gamblin' man?' Elias asked, lazily.

'Because my boss and enough men to take on an army is gonna come stormin' into Broken Man and wipe most of it out. All because of Red Carney.'

Creggan sat up to listen now. He knew more about that death than anyone else in the room. 'Red Carney . . . awful shame. He died right there, where your feet are planted, Ringo. I saw him die.'

'Really! Well, Mister Carney, he thinks that you and McCoy helped Red along the road to the next world.'

Creggan slammed the table. 'He's lyin', and he's just let all this eat away at him. Red Carney died of some sweatin' disease . . . a fever. The Doc said so. Even his golden medicine couldn't help. It was a natural death, I'm tellin' ya!'

Will came to the bars and spat out his answer, 'Sure, natural as a shot in the back! But in a few hours, you tin stars are due to be juicin' up that dead soil at the bone-yard!' He gave a deep, throaty laugh and waited for a response, but they ignored him.

They should have listened. A few miles away, Carney's men were now ready to leave. They were mounted and armed, and Itch had finally fought off his feeling of weakness, though his chest, as he sat and gave out the orders from the back of his pinto, still felt tight and there were spasms of pain down his back. He forced a laugh and then spoke to them all.

'Now boys, we're missin' Joe Dane and Will. I'm told that our Will is in the jail, so that changes the thinking some. Means we'll have to approach this more careful like. I want twelve men to storm into the place through the back wall.' He pointed at six men who were together at one end, holding lances, and another six with axes slipped into their saddles.

'See Jem and the boys there . . . they have these lances like the British cavalry. Only these is from my wood-yard . . . tougher than any lat of wood on a wall. Jem and the boys will just crash through the walls with these, and then the others – that's another half dozen – I want to have ready with axes.

The rest of us will hit the front door. We have surprise on our side, there's no time for them to think and react.'

What he meant was that Will could be a hostage. But the six men with the lances and the others with their axes would crack down the wall and be into the jail in seconds. He explained, 'When you six take the cells, get out quick with Will and lie flat. See, we'll all be annihilating the room. The thing is to make the holes with the points of lances, then get hacking straightaway with the axe blades. The sound alone will terrify the men inside, believe me!'

Everyone knew that there was some risk in this, and Carney spoke for them all when he said, 'Will has let us down bad, boys, and so we'll just have to risk him a mite. It's his own darned fault.'

17

Lydia was out early, before the family stirred, and she was dressed in anything but feminine attire. In fact, she was in a man's clothes, and would have been mistaken for such until the onlooker was close up. She wore a loose shirt and trousers, taken from her brother, and wore high boots. Tucked into her belt was a .28 calibre pocket revolver. She had read about revenge: it was in the most exciting stories in the books and periodicals, but now it was a real emotion, wracking her body like a fever.

By the time she reached The False Start the workers were stirring, and when they saw who it was, asked her what she was doing there so early. Lydia explained that she was there to see Harry.

Knowing that Harry was in bed with Miss Perdy, the staff tried to lie that he had left town. They were sensitive to the young woman's feelings, and everybody knew about her affection for the Englishman. But no sooner were the words spoken than Lydia saw Harry on the balcony, coming out of a bedroom, naked to the waist, stretching and humming a tune. Lydia called out his name and ran up the stairs.

Harry darted back in the room, where Perdy lay under the sheets, about to move into her day's activities, and he took his shirt and put it on, just as Lydia burst into the room. Her look was one of disgust, flashing her glance to each in turn, she pulled a sour face and lashed out the words, 'Lord Harry . . . you have . . . you have . . . how could you do this?'

Her dream had cracked like an old mirror. Her Bonneville was just like all the rest. He was no better than Joe Dane. In her mind, she had marked him out to be her special man. Harry understood all this, but as Lydia ran out, screeching her anger, he stopped to put on his boots, and by the time he was ready to pursue the girl, she was out of sight.

Lydia was rushing around the side-streets, looking for some place to hide and cope with her feelings, which were like a storm inside her. Something in her wanted to take that gun and spray bullets around at all the high walls. But no, if Harry wasn't the man to help revenge her father, then she would have to do it herself. It was a case of finding Joe Dane. Until she knew where he was, she would have to hide, and she headed for the Hoyts' makeshift church. There she ran to a shaded corner and sat, nursing her grudge and the barrel of the revolver. When folk stirred, she would ask after Joe.

*

At the jail, Creggan had not ignored Will Ringo and he took his concerns across to The False Start. There, Harry and Perdy were now up and moving around, with Harry wondering where the girl would be. But all thoughts of her vanished when Creggan told his tale.

'Perdy . . . Mister Lacey, sir . . . I think Will Ringo is speaking the truth. I think we should make ready for Carney and his men. It's well known he wants McCoy dead. I guess this is the day he does something, rather than his usual talk.'

McCoy was also dressed now and walking towards the jail, so he was called across. There was a council of war. But Harry wanted no part of it. He went to gather his bags and belongings ready for the stage which would soon be there. He tried to push things from his mind. If he went looking to find and help the girl, he would be back in the thick of trouble again, and if he joined the lawmen, he would have to kill maybe . . . and carry a gun again. It was best, he reasoned, to get out of town.

As Harry was about ready to sit and wait for the stage outside the stores, he saw McCoy and his men walk across to the jail. Then there was a sound of voices and movement around the main saloon of The False Start. There was a commotion, and some worried noises coming from a gathering crowd. Other people arrived, walking across the streets towards the place, looking around furtively. But Harry sat apart and said to himself, 'You are Lord Harry Lacey. You are not a gunman. You will move on and keep up the new life.'

But around him the familiar sense of panic was escalating: it was something he knew well from his former life, and he had prayed and sworn not to revert to the life of the gun. So many times had he sensed that shiver of expectancy which ran through anyone near to an imminent confrontation. It was almost as if there was adrenalin pumping through the general body of townsfolk, even the ones who never confront a criminal or respond to an open threat to their peace.

Still he sat there, like a statue, unmoved, or so it appeared – but through his mind there ran a storm of mixed images, from the shooting of young Lydia to the grey-faced corpse of Happen Boodle, who would now be at Doc Potworthy's in his coffin, with the burial expected tomorrow.

Fate had other things in mind, though, for Lord Harry. He was suddenly aware of someone at the end of the side street a few hundred yards from where he sat, and then the voice of Chet Two Winds hollered out 'Lord Harry . . . we need you!' This was followed by the voice of Hal Bornless, 'Yeah, I'm awful sorry I called you a liar. . . .'

Harry turned, still not saying a word. They both advanced towards him, then stopped close. Chet spoke first. 'Lord Harry, the sounds around Broken

Man say it all, more powerfully than any human voice: there's trouble coming, big trouble. Sheriff McCoy and his men are holed up in the jailhouse, expecting Carney and a very large number of gunmen. Basically, I need to recruit as many useful men as possible . . . and in about ten minutes. Most of all, we need a plan. We can't face 'em. We're out-numbered real high. I can't even tell you the figures. But Itch Carney, he's got around maybe a hundred hands. . . .'

'He's stretching facts as usual, my Lord . . . there's maybe fifty of 'em, all loco and boozed up.'

Harry was not going to shift on this. His face was stony, resolved. He had made a vow. But then there was another voice – the voice of a woman. From behind, he heard Perdy Candle say, 'Harry, I need you to stop a mess o' killing! I need you to stop this town slidin' into chaos. There's two men there hate each other, and dozens are likely to die if they're not stopped!'

She walked closer and now he saw her face clearly. The sun was rising now, and it was close to mid-day. Before Harry could answer, he was aware of a whole crowd of folks now, down the street, coming his way. In seconds they had huddled up into a crowd in front of him, and now the literary club looked more like a bunch of school kids than a gaggle of culture fiends.

'You know why I've brought everyone out to you here, Lord Harry!' This was Preacher Hoyt. 'We can't talk any longer . . . there's no time. I only want to say, I know you have told your soul that there is a bond that you will not kill again . . . after Hal told us about the pieces on you in the papers, I read them. There's a lot more to it than a change of heart, Lord Harry . . . you had a Road to Damascus moment, sir!'

'Now don't press it too far. That's not the case. I'm sorry to say that the Lord had nothing to do with my shooting of that girl . . . and the men. That was down to the man who used to be me. . . .'

'For heaven's sake . . . are you going to help us or not?' This was Mrs Hoyt.

'Fine. These are my terms. I will not carry a gun. But I want you all to obey orders and get started on it now.' They nodded. Something inside Harry Lacey had prompted him to act, to stick to his principles but to do the right thing now.

'OK. I want Sheriff McCoy in The False Start. Chet . . . do that now. You have a silver tongue, and also, tell him a small army is coming to crush his jail and that should persuade him. Perdy . . . get in the bar and barricade the front door with tables and chairs. Mr Bornless and Doc . . . get some men and have three wagons driven across the street at this side of the jail . . . I want a complete barricade there.'

Everyone darted around like rats scurrying for cover. McCoy was half-way back to his office when he was collared by Chet and some others. By now it was bright and warm, and everything was easy to see around the town. Joe Dane had now crept out of his dark corner of a yard, and was moving along the sides of the buildings along the side streets leading to the main road. From there he saw the wagons being driven into place, and after a quick look around, he saw a horse tethered nearby. That would be his best move, he thought, to ride around the long route to the other side of the jail, and meet up with Carney when he and his men arrived.

But then the unexpected happened: there was McCoy, striding across the street towards The False Start. It was the kind of luck that comes a man's way when things seem desperate.

It was an opportunity not to be missed. To make things even easier, McCoy stopped to talk to a deputy, with Chet Two Winds still there, nagging at him to get out of the street. It was going to be one of the plainest resolutions he had ever done – plain and simple. Dane took his revolver and aimed for McCoy's belly, but in a split second, the sheriff turned around and his back suddenly became the target. It would have to do. Two shots there should puncture both lungs. He would have no chance of survival.

Crouching behind some steps, Dane levelled the barrel at McCoy and pulled the trigger, and that hit home, but before he pulled again, his hand hit a railing and the second shot only hit the man's shoulder. Heads turned towards where the smoke had been seen, and he knew he would have to move real fast. He sprinted for the tethered horse and dug in his heels, turning it around ready for a swift exit. It was a beautiful young mustang, and its owner was now running out of the stores, cursing him.

In half a minute Joe Dane was urging his mount to full speed, heading out of town to the south, away from the trouble; he would arch around, as he had planned, and turn up in the right place.

McCoy was now bleeding and struggling to breathe, but Chet and two other men carried him inside the saloon to the Doc. Chet could see that there was a chance he would survive and he told him so. He knew that encouraging words were essential in that kind of situation. By now, the barricade was in place and Hal Bornless gathered some townsfolk to stand along the carriages and wagons. He shouted for some rifles, and the store-keeper brought some out, just in time to hear the sound of horses' hoofs coming closer, on the San Pedro road. It was a drumming, threatening noise, like something that would usually be heard on a battlefield. Everyone strained to listen at first: Perdy and Harry in The False Start, now with the Doc working hard on extracting the bullet from McCoy's shoulder, and the deputies in the jailhouse.

Will, still behind the bars inside, started laughing. There was Elias Hole and Creggan, with two other deputies, still at the table, but they heard the drumming noise too and they stood up and went to the windows. 'See, I told you . . . prepare to exit the world, gentlemen . . . say some prayers!' Will said this with torment, as if he were twisting a blade in a wound. Elias told him to shut up and dragged a small table across the door. Then he and the others took hold of the solid, long table in the middle of the room, and pushed that across one of the windows.

'It's a siege, like in the olden days!' Elias said. 'Remember that we got protection. They're out in the open air. Numbers aren't so crucial.'

There was one other observer of course: Lydia had moved silently and quickly out of the church, and she saw the sheriff fall as well, though she couldn't see Joe Dane. But she went silently as a hunter, around the back of The False Start, climbing into a back room after smashing a small window. All she wanted was Joe, and she knew that by listening and watching, the time would come when he was in her sight.

She saw and heard Harry stand up now and carry on with his orders. 'Right, we have three men armed at the windows. Perdy, you have no weapon?'

'Oh yeah . . . a little pocket pistol. I can take one out if he comes a little closer.'

'Now, look, there's one obvious ploy here. Let me try it.' Harry walked to the front door and slid a table out of the way, stepping outside. As he looked along the street towards the jail, beyond the barricade he could now see a line of hats, and the

137

drumming of the horses on the move had stopped. Heads turned to look at him as he walked towards the wagons, and Chet shouted for him to get back inside. But he squeezed between two wagons and walked calmly out into the sun.

Harry had taken three steps when Carney shouted for him to freeze. 'I don't know who you are, but you're more fool than a stage clown, mister. You wanna die today?' Carney had just been ready to shout for the charge, and the men behind were riding very close to the back wall.

Harry had to raise his voice, as he was a hundred yards away from Carney. 'Mr Carney, I have to tell you that Sheriff McCoy is dead. We believe that Joe Dane killed him. I think that's all you wanted today. How about you turn around and go home?'

'Well it used to be, and that's the best news in years, if it's true . . . but you see, first I have to see his body, and second, I need to destroy that damned jail anyway, so scuttle back inside, you madman . . . you have no weapons I see. Who the hell are you?' He turned to his line of men and asked, 'Anybody fancy an easy target?' Someone fired at Harry's feet, just out of bravado, and the bullet spit dust, but Harry never moved an inch.

This could have gone well, except that out of sight, behind the jail, the men with the lances and axes heard the gun shot and went into action. There was a noise loud enough to awaken the dead, as first the points smashed into timber, and then the axes followed, with a fusillade of rifle shots higher, over the barred window. It was an immediate sign for Elias and Creggan to open fire, and their bullets picked off two of Carney's men.

There was no going back. The nine men opened fire with their Winchesters in return of fire, and a terrifying volley of hot metal thumped and crashed into the jail wall and through the windows. Two deputies and Creggan fell dead, leaving Elias alone, now cowering behind the big table, with shots ringing out in front of him and axes and bullets hacking and splintering the jail wall behind.

In another minute, Carney's men were inside and they shook hands with Will Ringo. They all turned to look at Elias, who stood alone, facing them, a pistol in one hand and a hunting knife in the other.

'Any of you men in the mood for a fight?' he snapped out. They all knew it would have been wrong just to gun him down, and before they could do or say anything, the main door was smashed open and in came enough men to overpower even a giant of a man like Elias. Carney shouted, 'Don't shoot him . . . just tie him up.' He was soon tied firmly at his wrists and ankles, and thrown into a corner.

Harry was back in the saloon now, and he was told that McCoy was most likely going to live. The sheriff was lying on Perdy's chaise longue, bandaged, stinking of whiskey and mumbling something about 'that

139

bastard cattleman. . . .'

'Ladies and gentlemen, we have a sheriff who is very much alive, and an army out there who want him dead.. ..' He rapped out more orders. 'You men . . . get Chet and the others back in here, right now!'

It didn't take long for everyone to be inside, and for Carney and his men, along the street, to start dismounting and plan the next move. But before Carney himself had dismounted and could give his orders, riding up behind came Joe Dane.

'Why, son, apparently you did the job. I'm told the swine who killed my brother is now lying in Satan's clutches. Well done, boy! We've been wonderin' where the hell you've been. Some of us thought you'd taken a bullet and was a dead man. I should have known my resolution man was bidin' his time before a strike, eh?'

'Sure. You hit it there, sir, that's my thinking.'

'Well, find yourself a spot, son. We need all available fire-power now.'

'Good, Mr Carney, very good. I will, but first there's our deal. I just need the rest of my money, and I'll be moving on.' Joe knew that he had been seen and that the law was now on his tail. He also knew that McCoy might not have died, and so did Carney. 'Wait a minute there, my resolution man . . . I have to see the corpse of the man first.'

Joe knew that there was nothing else for it but to go along with Carney, pretend to co-operate, but he stayed mounted as Carney and the rest went towards The False Start. Joe shouted that he would follow them, but his mind was working out possibilities, and he trailed behind, on the mustang, ready for a quick exit.

He needed one. At the barricade, Carney and his men took positions, all their attention fixed on the saloon, and from there, Harry waved a white kerchief and was told to walk out.

He stood there, still a man with no gun-belt and no rifle in his hands. Itch Carney stared at him in disbelief, as he stood behind a wagon tailboard and said, 'I have to ask again, who the hell are you, fella?' As he said this, he felt the spasm of pain in his chest again, and he staggered against the board. Will Ringo was by his side again, and he knew the signs. 'Hey boss . . . you sick again? You are, you got the heart trouble, I know it boss.'

But Carney, screwing up his face, listened to the stranger, ignoring Will.

'I am Lord Harry Lacey, Mr Carney, and I have to tell you that the man you want is in here . . . but my earlier words were untrue. In fact, he lives. Sheriff McCoy is alive, though your man very nearly finished him, let me tell you.'

'Yes, but who the hell are you?' Carney clutched at his chest now. He had to sit, and Will offered some whiskey.

'I'm a man of law. That sums me up, sir.'

Though sick and in pain, Itch Carney laughed.

141

He laughed so much that his words could be heard some distance away, and in her back room, Lydia heard him say, 'A Lord? An actual old-fashioned Lord, did you say? Well, I have to congratulate you. Somehow you stopped Joe Dane taking out the old sheriff. You hear that, Joe?' He raised his voice even more. The pain was wearing off.

'Yes, sir. Can I finish him now?'

Lydia heard that familiar voice, and her hand tightened on the grip of her revolver. Could she get around behind him? Maybe not.

Harry was still standing in the open. 'Now Mr Carney, I'm told that McCoy was the target today. I understand that you would walk away from here if the man was dead. Is that right?'

'That's all I want, mister. But here ain't no corpse in there you say, so I'm afraid my boys is gonna have to come in and plug the heathen.'

'Like I told you, sir, I'm a man of law. That means I have to do my best to prevent you from committing such a heinous murder. You have to get past me.'

Carney laughed again, and so did the bunch of gunmen ranged behind him, all behind the wagons. 'Say, Lacey ... how many guns you got in there then? Six? The women armed too? Now see, you ain't even armed. I could finish you now.'

From behind came the distinct voice of Perdy Candle, who now walked out to stand with Harry.

It was all too much for Joe Dane. He could see

that he was never going to get the man nor the money. His brain told him that the best move was to ride away, and he turned quietly around and cantered off, towards the Big Question, telling Carney that he was hurt – which indeed he was, as anyone could see. The old man didn't care one rotten carcass about what Joe Dane wanted. No, it was time to take, not to wait around for the impossible.

His words were clear enough for Lydia to hear, and she stole away to borrow a horse from the stables behind. Never in her life did she ever think that one day she would be hunting Joe Dane – tracking him, and with a gun ready to use against him. Part of her was thinking that sometimes the stories in the books worked into life itself, and it was more scary than a disturbed grizzly.

18

Harry Lacey's head was spinning, as he racked his brain to think of the best strategy. But he saw that there was no other way than the way of the gun. He could see that Perdy had now distracted Carney, and he walked back inside, and asked for a belt and a Colt from Chet. 'What? What you aimin' to do, Harry?'

'I'm aiming to trample on all my resolve, and try to save some lives.'

But Perdy's appearance was having its effect, and Carney sensed the turmoil in his breast as the emotions swamped him. This was the woman he wanted to marry; now she was standing in his way, stopping him from doing what he had yearned to do for so long – take the life of the man who had killed his own kin.

'Perdy . . . please go away . . . go somewhere else! I have to see that man die. I came here today with a battle in mind. I was prepared to kill anyone who stood in my way, but by God I can't hurt you. . . .'

'Itch, the man has only one lung. He's still bleed-ing too much. The Doc's maybe saved him, but he'll never be a sheriff again . . . never be the same man at all. I'm begging you to forget all the rancour, all that spite and the hunger for vengeance, and turn around . . . go back to your home. Please, Itch . . . if you ever loved me!'

The words had some kind of effect. Carney soft-ened for a moment. But before he could reply, a relentless, deep surge of pain shot through him. He dropped his rifle and both hands went to his chest, and he fell heavily to the ground. Will Ringo ran over and loosened his boss's collar, asked if he was all right, but saw sweat pouring from the cattle-man's brow: his face seemed to change hue, and he groaned Perdy's name. She heard this and ran to him, squatting over him, calling his name. There was a shudder through Carney's body, and then he was still, his arms falling by his side.

'Boss! Boss!' Will Ringo yelled, and shook his master's body, as if that would bring him back. Someone shouted for Doc Potworthy, and he was soon there, standing over Carney; then laying a finger on the man's wrist, he said solemnly, 'He's dead, Perdy, he's dead.'

'What about Joe Dane?' Chet Two Winds asked the world in general, 'and come to that, what about Elias – where's he? What happened in the jail-house?'

'Joe Dane went out to the Big Question,' Will said. Harry knew that it was his job to bring the man in. 'I'll go get him,' he said, 'I'll bring him in. He almost killed McCoy.'

Chet brought up his own horse. 'I'll come with you, Harry . . . take my mount. I'll get another and follow you . . . get going before the man heads out for that endless plain out there!'

'Sure. I think it's time we had Preacher Hoyt here, folks. It's his turn now.' As he rode off, Harry could see poor Perdy, still weeping over Itch Carney's body.

Joe Dane had gone out to the Big Question, and his plan was obvious to anyone who might sit down and think about the man and what he was like. His reasoning was predictable: if he wasn't going to have the rest of the money, then he was going to take what he could. He knew, with the instinct of a die-hard rogue, that as the private army of cowpokes was in town, the place would be all but deserted – and sure enough, as he rode in, an old-timer came out to greet him with, 'It's you, Dane . . . is it all over in town? Did he git McCoy?'

Joe followed his instincts. There was no time for chatter and pretence: that was too risky. He pulled his gun out quick as a whip and shot the man dead in a matter of seconds. Another man inside the house came rushing out, pointing a rifle at him, but Joe shot a bullet into his head before he could find the trigger with his finger. After that everything seemed dead still, like a grave-yard.

He tethered the horse, and with his rifle ready to fire, he walked steadily through the rooms of the main house, looking for a safe and for any valuable that might be apparent to a trained eye like his. Thieving came as naturally to him as taking lives. It was all part of being a man untroubled by scruples – indeed, scruples were the heaviest burden a man could have weighing on him, far more irksome than a pack or a sack.

Dane looked hard wherever he found himself, but there was no sign of any safe. Where would a man with all the wealth of Itch Carney keep his money? Maybe, he thought, he was one of the careful types who bought diamonds and stored them. His head was full of maybes.

What he did not know was that Lydia Santo had arrived at the ranch as well, and she was on his trail. After finding the second body, she sensed that, strangely, she was hunting the hunter. Every tissue in her body, every sense, strained as she listened for the slightest sound. She was racking her brain, wondering why he would come there. It had to be that he was owed, that there was something for him. But that was not the most important thing for her: no, the man who had killed her father was now somewhere in these buildings. That was all that mattered.

Finally, Dane reached a wide sitting room, and there were shelves and classy looking armchairs and stools; there were paintings on the wall, mostly of horses, and there was a portrait of Richard Carney, most likely Itch Carney's father, looking as though he owned more land than he could ride over in a day; he was dressed like a state governor or some big noise back East.

For a while he was distracted by this, but then he noticed the safe in the corner, on a stand below a cupboard. It had some kind of double lock, and that was, or could have been, a problem. But not for Joe Dane: for him, bullets solved just about every riddle that fate put in front of a man. With no hesitation, he fired three bullets into the lock. There was a shattering of metal and some shards flew across the room, just missing his cheek. With a satisfied smile, he went down on his knees and wrenched the door open. There were several piles of notes and some rings in there, and he almost whooped with delight when he saw them. But he suddenly started back, like a rabbit hearing the fox breaking sticks as it walked up behind. In this case, it was a trigger being cocked.

'So, Joe Dane is as skilful a robber as he is a killer. Take the guns from both holsters and throw them across this lovely rich carpet, mister.'

He didn't turn, but did as she asked. The best option in a tight corner like this was to shut up, sit tight and bide your time. He had always been slippery enough to wriggle out of most tight corners, and this was only a girl who threatened.

'Now turn around, with your arms up in the air, and get to your feet.' He did as he was told, and as he turned to look at her, he smiled. 'Why, Lydie . . . you know I'm all mixed up in my head now. You see, I thought you was thinkin' to run off with me . . . as my wife. That was always our plan.'

'Shut up, Joe. I know what you did. It's time to pay.'

'Ah now, Lydie, it was never meant to come to this! Don't you believe in destiny? We were destined to be man and wife, with our own land . . . children, money . . . you see what's in this safe? I reckon there's around six thousand dollars in there. Enough for you and me to live like rich folks . . . you always like the opera, the poets, all that nonsense. Well, you could have all that. Just put the gun down.'

She ignored every word and simply spat out the words that had nagged and tugged at her since she ran from home with the gun, 'Joe Dane, you killed my father. Justice has caught up with you.'

He was now thinking that his chances of surviving this were thin. It was an animal response. He threw himself at her, and her finger pulled the trigger as he flapped an arm at her and then slammed into her roughly, knocking her to one side and flat on the floor. The bullet went into the ceiling.

The sound of the bullet brought the other hunter to the room too: Harry Lacey was only a minute's walk away, and he rushed to the source of the shot. But caution was built into him as natural as blood and he paused outside the room, as he heard voices and then the sound of a struggle. As he reached the door, Lydia fell through the doorway and he caught her. Before she could say a word, Harry saw Joe Dane ahead of him, bending to pick up his revolver. He had grabbed it and was pointing the barrel at Lydia when Harry saw the situation and she was shoved aside out of danger. The bullet hit Harry in the arm. Lydia screamed, 'Watch out, Harry!'

But Joe Dane stopped for a second and said, 'Ah, I heard about you. Harry, eh? Lord Harry Lacey? Well now, I killed so many varieties of men you know, but never no blue-blooded English fancy Lordy type of dude. There's always a first time.'

He stepped backwards to the end of the room and asked Harry to come in. Harry, his hand hovering over his Colt, went in carefully.

'Now, Harry Lordy man, we're gonna have a traditional shoot-up. That is, I have two revolvers here and I see that you are armed also, so we're gonna draw. You a handy type with a gun, Harry Lordy? I hope so, or there's likely to be a noxious stink of death in this very nice, civilized room.'

'Keep back there, Lydia . . . keep well away!' Harry shouted. His wounded arm throbbed with pain. Sadly it was his better hand for drawing from his holster.

They faced each other. Harry's mind went back to

those times, so many of them, when he had faced the little upstarts who had heard about him, been told his reputation, and had come looking for him, wanting to take him on. He had thought his life had seen an end to all that; he had thought he had put a stop to the senseless killings, the pointless confrontations. But what rushed back into him was also the keen, quick as lightning flick of a wrist that was required. He looked deeply into Dane's eyes. That was part of the face-off as well: the play of the minds, the strength of will and the resolve to come away the victor. He saw a killer, but he saw the fear as well.

'Go when you like, Englishman.' Dane's smile was forced, sweat-lined, a touch too artificial. There were hands darting down the inches to the grips, and then the dual lift of the lethal weapons. Then there were cracks as bullets ripped out and over the warm air of the room and into something that had no chance of resistance. In this case, it was flesh.

That flesh was the chest of Joe Dane. He called out what was meant to be, 'Die, Lacey . . .' but it was never completed. His fall took him back and his head cracked on a sturdy wooden shelf. He fell down, life seeping out of him.

Lydia rushed in and looked at the body of the man she had hunted, then rushed to Harry Lacey and fell at his feet. 'Lord Harry . . . thank God you're all right! You did it, you did it . . . for me!'

Harry now sat down, with Lydia still holding him,

this time his wounded arm. She saw that the bullet had nipped the flesh and gone through.

'No, Lydia. Not for you. It was justice. I thought ... I thought it existed without life being taken, without the shame of it all!'

'Shame?' She looked up at him, puzzled. 'There's nothing shameful about revenge. He killed my father ... my real father, Harry. You evened everything up, and it's settled.'

'Settled? I wish I could believe that. I guess vows are meant to be broken. Life tends to step in and make a liar of us.'

They stayed out there for quite a while, and eventually an old man came out of a barn along the way, and walked stealthily towards them. He was crouching as he came near, and then seemed to relax as he saw that the noise he had heard appeared to have stopped. He was round and plump, with a distinctive Texan drawl, and he wore an apron over his ragged pants and torn, stained shirt. He was bald and shiny on the head, and his face broke into a smile when he saw Lydia.

'Why, what was all that row? This man dead, is he? You shot him?'

'Who are you mister?' Harry asked, still half expecting the man to have a pistol tucked into his belt on the other side of the belly.

'I beg your pardon sir. I'm Cal Mildew ... Mr Carney knew me as Corney. I was his cook. Truth is, I sneaked back in here last night. He threw me out a while back. Didn't like my chow.'

'You don't know what's being going on then, Corney?' Lydia asked.

'Well, I know that some wild man arrived here and shot dead two of my *amigos*. I saw it . . . it was this heap of offal here at your feet. As runnin' is better than fightin' you see, I ran for the blackest corner of the old barn and lay down with the mules. I may be three score and ten, and livin' on borrowed time a mite, but I'd like to keep my blood in my body some time longer, you understand.'

Harry was puzzled as to why Carney would let a man like this go from his outfit. He was entertaining, to say the least. 'Mildew, do you think you could make this young lady and myself a meal . . . something simple and substantial? Because I'm not ready to move back to town yet.'

Corney Mildew was only too pleased to do it. He beamed with pleasure. 'Just you sit there and nurse that wound, mister, and I'll make a meal fit for a king. . . .'

'He's only a lord,' Lydia said.

'Well, I know what kings eat, but I can't say I ever fed a lord . . . like a real English kind of lord.'

'Oh, we eat everything that other folks eat. Somethin' hot and sharp maybe.'

Mildew made himself busy, and he knew the ranch well enough to gather everything he needed. It was an appearance at exactly the right moment for Harry Lacey. He had been knocked back, forced

153

to revise everything he had believed in since he began that new life. As Lydia made him sit still in a roomy armchair, she wrapped the wound. Though only a nick, there was blood enough. She let him rest and she busied herself with Corney when he called for her to help.

Harry was not ready to move at all. The day had been a severe test of his courage as well as of his will. He sat still and let his mind rove across time and place, trying to understand what had happened. The bottom line was plain: he had killed to avoid being killed, and for sure, the rat was sure to have put a bullet in the girl, or maybe run off with her. But what really set him back was the fact that he had drawn against a proven killer, and he had finished the man, even with his own best hand unable to move normally. He had overcome his sense of morality and eclipsed it with another morality. Whispering to himself he said, 'So, Harry Lacey, the arms of justice have to be stronger than the bad men.'

Was he seeing himself afresh, now that he was too exhausted to walk or ride? Had he ever really known himself?

Soon the three of them sat down to eat, at the long, solid table of Itch Carney. Corney Mildew had only a few teeth and he apologized for the rough approach to chewing beef he had to adopt. He told the story of why he had left the Big Question, and how he and Itch had been partners many years back, starting out with just a few beasts and Red Carney's skill in business. 'He sure missed that brother of his, Lord Harry.'

'Is it true that McCoy was responsible for Red's death?' Lydia asked.

'Truth is, Mr Carney talked himself into seeing that as the fact. I don't know. All I know is, this place went from bad to worse as soon as Itch was taken bad. You know, when a man is sick, he tends to hit out at everything, even the ones he claims to have some affection for. Shame he went to his death knowin' he'd thrown out his oldest *compadre* . . . my good self!'

With full bellies and no sense of rushing, the three of them took to the road back to town, with Corney singing old ballads all the way, and their mounts never going beyond a steady trot. Harry thought it was strange, but he was sure that Lydia had been reading his mind. She said, suddenly and out of nowhere, 'You know, Harry, I can see now that I made you a knight from my storybooks . . . I'm sorry for that. Was I too much of a pest?'

'Like a meat fly around a shiny stallion!' he said and then laughed so loud that she saw the teasing and joined in.

Back in Broken Man, when they rode in, Elias Hole had been found and freed of his shackles, and Preacher Hoyt and the literary club had agreed that he would be the ideal sheriff if McCoy couldn't work again – and the signs were that he would never be more than a shell of the man he once was.

Harry dismounted and was greeted by his new friends from the club and The False Start. When he saw Alby Groot he said, 'Mr Groot, there's at least three corpses out there at the Big Question in need of your professional attention.'

Alby thought it was bad form to smile or look pleased in any way, but he did feel like rubbing his hands. Then the thought struck him that there was nobody to pay for the burials and the coffins, and he had to ask himself why he had ever come out to this unwelcoming frontier.

In The False Start that night, Perdy managed to raise enough strength to sing along with the band, and it was free drinks for all. Harry sat in a quiet corner, taking in some strong drink and trying to handle the feelings that were overpowering him. But all in all, he told himself, though he had taken a life, he had saved many. Most of all, he had saved the life of a young girl, and years back he had taken such a life. Some potent working of fate tends to even things out, he thought. Then in the midst of this soul-searching there was a lull, and he found himself facing a deputation: it was the literary club. Hal Bornless, journalist and lecturer, entertainer and jester, spoke for them all.

'Mr Lord Harry Lacey, on behalf of the Broken Man Literary Club of Colorado, I wish to thank you for coming all the way out here, where most of the refinements of cultured life tend to hit the buffers, and I want to humbly apologise for digging up the dirt on your past life as a gunslinger because I see now that you consider such a life debases a man . . . and, well, to cut a long speech short, we would like you to stay around a while and maybe do some more lecturing and so on . . . failing that, you could run the place, because we never saw a man take charge with such authority.'

'Yes,' added Chet, 'and it also must be said that we're all mighty glad you had that violent past, my Lord. Sometimes a man's natural talents have to come through . . . and fortunately for us, Joe Dane and a few others got in your way!'

'I'm very flattered, everyone, I surely am. But the events at the Big Question turned out to be the most ironical in my life. I did ask myself a big question after that shooting – the biggest of them all. What to do with your life. Well, in my case, it's going to have to be a life with this again.' He looked down to his waist, where his tough leather belt now held two revolvers. 'If you still want to pay me for the lecture, I'd be happy to take a horse instead of cash.'

Preacher Hoyt was reminded that he had a fine bay mare that hardly ever went out beyond his paddock, and he took the hint and sent for it. He was still feeling mean for not paying the man his fee, and the horse was one he had been given after a family death.

Harry thanked them all, and explained why he was now a gunslinger again, but not so plainly. He had to lift the edge of his coat to show his belt and guns.

'I bought these today . . . Frontier Colt Double Action . . . like I always had. Good friends if needed. I have a hankering to do some lawman work . . . but not around here. You got this young lady's father for that. I think Elias Hole could be one excellent tin star sheriff.' He looked across to the door, where Lydia had just come in. She heard what he said, and came to shake his hand. She wouldn't have spoken a word about it, but she had never, until that day, been filled with a certainty that she would, some time soon, become the Liza di Buco of her dreams.

When she shook that hand and gave him a big, affectionate smile, inside she was thinking *You could have been my Bonneville . . . maybe you still are*, but what she actually said was 'I want to thank you, Lord Harry Lacey, and wish you the best. Will you come around this way again soon?'

'Sure. Might not be soon, but I'll be riding into this main street again, and I expect you to be runnin' the show and barkin' out orders.'

The mare arrived and was given to him, saddled and ready. 'I'm calling her Lydie,' Harry said, 'Now you go and make that romantic dream come true, young lady!' He felt a disturbing shiver of memory come over him, as it was so long since he had ridden out, alone, with nothing but leather, fire-power and a strong horse beneath him, waiting for the dig of his heels.

The new day was the hottest of the year, and as folk were still working to clear up the mess and think about burying their dead, Harry Lacey, with the superb new bay mare given him by the literary society under him, rode out of Broken Man, his thoughts still diving between past and the possible future. So, the pretenders and gun-crazy kids might come looking for him, but in the end, justice needed to *match* the wrong-doers, not only look on them with contempt.

He turned and took one last look at Broken Man. Then he said to himself, *what a borderland . . . just like the one I have inside me somewhere. . . .* He had to believe, as he rode into an uncertain future, that he knew himself better now.